THE PARLAY

Tomas M. DeLaCruz

This is a work of fiction. Names, characters, businesses, events and incidents either are the product of the author's imagination or are used fictitiously, and any resemblance to actual persons, living or dead, or locales is entirely coincidental.

The Parlay

Chapter 1

The life I lived was because of greed and curiosity. That is what I told myself as I watched my life unfold before my eyes. The amount of happiness that conquered me during my quest made me who I am, but it also was what controlled me. It made me do unheard-of things, and I regret some of those decisions. But I am glad that I experienced them too.

I had everything a man could ask for in his life. Now look at you, such a disappointment and a failure.

Behold, this is my story of how I became who I am and the price I paid for living the life I did:

My name is Will, Will Bigsley, and I was born just outside St. Paul, Minnesota. My father was a foundry worker; he would leave early morning and come home a little past evening from work.

My mother worked for a sewing company, and she only worked so many hours out of the day and came home to cook and care for the house.

Every night after dinner, I would sit with my father; he had sports on and watched whatever was on tv that night. Even though I knew nothing about sports, I would still sit with him and watch his every emotion as he yelled or cheered at the tv.

After many years, I graduated from high school, and it was my turn to venture into reality. The lessons from my parents and school hopefully gave me the experience I need for what's next in life.

I met a beautiful lady by the name of Karina after my graduation, and we decided to move out of Minnesota. We found ourselves leaving the cold wintery state for an overheated condition. We landed in the city of Kingman, Arizona. Beautiful scenery, with many opportunities to become someone in life. We tried college, but after a couple of years of being here, Karina became pregnant, and I needed a job to keep the money coming in.

We found out our baby was a girl and named her Ashley. Our decision for care was that Karina would be a stay-at-home mom, and I would work to support us. I had started my career as a line cook at a small restaurant, and the pay wasn't great, so I had left there searching for something different.

Next job, I was in human resources for a small factory. That job seemed great until the owner sold his company and closed his doors.

The amount of stress I received jumping from job to job was exhausting. Then I came across a dealership that was in search of a salesman. I wanted to turn it down, but Karina kept pushing me to go for it.

"This seems like a great opportunity for you, and maybe you even can further your career down the line," Karina said.

We had our debates about the job, but I realized I needed to work, and this one was right in front of me. So, I decided to go for it.

Auto Haven is the name of the dealership. The place's owner is Blake Fenningway, and he owns three dealerships in Arizona. One dealership is in Kingman, another is in Henderson, and the more prominent dealership is in Las Vegas.

Every week, Blake would send me to Las Vegas to check in on his dealership to oversee the manager and how he had everything going. On my way to the dealership, I stop at a coffee stand for some coffee; there's a building that says 'Place Your Bets Here' on the window. I'm not one for sports or gambling, so I never go there. I stand there and watch people come in and out of the building while I drink my coffee. I am curious about what is in there, but I am on a time crunch from the mission the boss man gave me.

The store manager in Las Vegas is a nephew of Blake's, which Blake gave him as a favor. I don't think he had any prior knowledge of selling cars before getting the job. Still, the dealership is the money maker for us. I would head over there to count stock and ensure our inventory is correct. After completing the task, I head back to Kingman and give the boss my data.

Once I get back to the dealership, I head inside. Blake usually sits in his office on his computer if he isn't with anyone. It's essentially his home away from home in the office. I entered his office and gave him my papers; this time was a little different. He had asked me something that would change my life forever.

"Will, do you like to gamble?" Blake asked me.

I responded, "I'm not much of a gambler, sir. I have yet to step inside a casino since moving here."

Blake stopped what he was doing on the computer and closed his eyes. He said as he opened his eyes, "What if I took you to a casino? It wouldn't be for long since I know you have a family waiting at home for you. Maybe for an hour or two, and we would come back."

I tilted my head back and thought, is it a brilliant idea for me to go? "I am sorry, sir, but I would need to ask my girlfriend to make sure she's okay with it."

"It is okay if you can't go. But whenever you decide that you want to journey into a casino, let me know, and I will take you, son."

As I was driving home, the only thing I could think of was the question the boss asked me. Why would he suddenly ask me that? I have been at the dealership for at least four years, and he has always been quiet about the casinos and gambling. Was he making conversation, or was there something going on?

I finally got home from what seemed like a long drive. As I opened the door, Ashley ran up to me and gave me a huge hug.

I said to Ashley, "What smells so good? Is mommy cooking?"

She nods with a smile and runs off to the kitchen. As I walked into the kitchen, I saw a pan of meatloaf that Karina had sitting on the stove with a pot of mashed potatoes next to it. I snuck up behind Karina, put my hands on her hips, and whispered, "This looks amazing and smells great!" Of course, sneaking up behind her, I slightly scare her and receive a cloth potholder to the face. We both laugh, and then she kisses me.

She asks, "How was work?"

I told her what I did and how the day went. Then I told her what the boss had asked me in the office about gambling and casinos.

Karina replied, "With everything going on and us just making it by, it wouldn't be a good idea to spend any extra money we don't have."

I nodded and said, "Yeah, you are right. I don't need to be out there when everything I need is here at home."

Karina smiled, pulled me closer to her, and gently kissed me. She put her arms on my shoulder, and the gentle kiss turned into an intimate kiss.

As she tenderly nibbled on my top lip, we heard Ashley say to us as she entered the kitchen, "Ewwww, you guys are kissing."

After we ate dinner, I told Karina, "Babe, why don't you sit back and relax. I'll wash the dishes and put them away for you."

Karina gazes into my eyes and says, "How did I ever get so lucky with a man like you? You work every day as I am home but still spoil me with loving gestures that steal my heart repeatedly." Karina gives me the tightest hug and walks away.

As she walks away, it is only suitable for a man to show his woman some love with a lovely soft slap on the butt cheek.

Karina looks back with a playful smile, then says, "Oh, you're going to get it later!"

Once done with the dishes and cleaning up, I get a phone call from Blake. I usually don't get a late-night call from the boss unless it is crucial, so I answered, "Hey, boss, what's up?" Karina looked at me with concern.

Blake answers, "Sorry to bother you late at night, but I need a huge favor from you. Can you open the dealership tomorrow without me? I have some business to deal with and will be in later."

"Of course, sir, I would be happy to do that."

"I knew I could count on you. The employee of the month, I can see it already."

I thought for a moment; we are the only two people working inside the dealership. It made me scratch my head for a bit.

Once I ended the call, Karina asked, "Is everything okay?"

I replied, "Yea, the boss wants me to open the dealership tomorrow because he has some business to handle. He'll arrive a little late from what he said."

Karina responded humorously, "Oooooooo, you will be the boss man for a couple of hours or more." Then she started to poke all over my body. She reached for my shirt to pull me close and added flirtatiously, "You know, that is super sexy!" Then she pulled my head down for a kiss and said, "I love you."

"I love you too, sugar plum."

Karina laughed, "You're a dork!"

"Ashley, time for bed!" Karina yelled out.

"But I'm not tired and want to stay up!" Ashley exclaimed.

Karina put her hands on her hips and glared at Ashely, "Okay young lady, you stayed up late yesterday. So, today you will need to go to bed so your sleeping schedule doesn't get messed up."

Ashely looks at Karina with puppy eyes, "Okay, can you and daddy tuck me in."

"Yes, I will be there to tuck you in," I said to Ashley. "But only if you beat me up the stairs." I started running up the stairs for a head start

Ashley yells, "Hey, no fair!" She follows behind me and beats me up the last couple of stairs.

"Ha! I win!" Ashley yells as she jumps onto her bed.

I tucked her in, kissed Ashley's forehead, and said, "Good night, princess." Karina enters and does the same. We turned off the light and closed the door.

Karina gazes into my eyes again and says, "You are the best dad and boyfriend ever." Then she gives me another tight hug.

The following day, I get to the dealership, and a mysterious man is leaning on the entrance door. He is wearing a black hoodie with the hood over his head and has on black sweatpants. I thought to myself, this can't be good. I took about five mins in my car to think about everything that could go wrong and right. Finally, I stepped out of my car and approached the mysterious man.

"Can I help you with something?!" I shouted out.

He replied, "I'm looking for Fenningway. Have you seen him?"

"No," I answered even though I knew he had some business to take care of from what the boss man told me last night. Is this man the reason why he isn't coming to work? Could he be in debt with someone or in trouble? Is this man going to harm me? All these things were racing through my head, then I continued, "He had some family issues to take care of."

The man reached behind him, and I instantly thought he was reaching for a gun. Am I going to get shot? What about my family? Is someone going to find my dead body if he must hide it? Why does it have to be me? So many things I was dwelling on during this event.

His hand comes back forward and is holding a small but bulky envelope. He starts walking toward me, and I am terrified to the extreme. He hands me the envelope and says, "Can you ensure Fenn gets this?" The man grinned and continued, "I would hate for something to happen to you if this package does not get to him."

"Okay, I will make sure he gets it."

The man walks away and gets into a shiny luxury vehicle. It looks like the vehicle was just detailed not that long ago. You could see the bright lights from the parking lot in the reflection. Maybe we should hire the guy that detailed this car from how nice it looked, I told myself as I laughed.

I took a deep breath from this near-death situation and unlocked the doors to the dealership. I turned on all the lights, changed the coffee filter and added more coffee to the pot. Turned it on, and immediately you could smell the brewing of the coffee. It is a refreshing smell that helps me wake up in the morning.

Once I completed my task list for the morning, I sat in my office with this package. Again, my mind is racing with so many questions. What is this package? Would he be mad at me if I opened it up? It wouldn't hurt anything if I peeked inside, right? Why did he have to take this morning off and leave me to manage this situation?

After a couple of hours went by, Blake entered the dealership. I greeted him and said, "Hey boss, how's it going? I have a package for you."

Blake replied, "Oh great, I've been awaiting it. Where is it at?"

"In my office. Do you want me to bring it to you?"

"I'll be in my office, so bring it to me there."

I grabbed it and started walking over to his office. Should I tell him about the guy outside in the morning waiting for him? I handed him the package and stood there like a little kid waiting for something.

"You can close my door on the way out," Blake said. "I want to be alone when I open this up, if that's okay."

I nodded and said, "Okay, I will be in the showroom if you need me." I walked out of his office, closed the door, and walked towards the showroom. A couple was looking at one of the luxury vehicles we had inside. I approached them and talked about the vehicle to see if they were interested in it.

After the couple left, I returned to my office and sat for a second. I looked at my phone and saw I had a voicemail and missed a call from Karina. I listened to the voicemail, and Karina said, "Hey there, handsome; I hope you have an amazing day today. Last night was unbelievable; I love nights when we make love like that."

I had already started my day off badly in my head, but hearing that voicemail brought a big smile. I closed my eyes and became lost in a daydream. I heard a voice say, "With that smile, you can brighten up a 3rd world country. It looks like someone had a little fun last night." I opened my eyes, and Blake was standing in the doorway with an enormous grin than I had.

After all that, Blake came into the office and closed the door. He sat down in a chair across from mine. He then asks, "How is everything at home doing? I remember you telling me that your girlfriend is a stay home mom. With her not working, do you guys have enough income to sit comfortably at home?"

As he was asking the questions, I had a blank look. I finally shook it off and replied, "Well.... we are just getting by. We aren't comfortable, but we have a good system that helps us."

Blake nodded and said, "Okay, good. It's always great to have that communication in a relationship. That package you gave me earlier had my winnings from the casino, and I didn't just win my money back; I won a jackpot betting on a couple of sports bets."

Blake pulled out a roll of $100 bills and continued, "With my help, this is why I want you to join me at the casino. You could be making this kind of investment."

I paused for a second and shook my head. I replied, "I don't want to mess up a system that works for us. What if I lose money and now the system doesn't work? Then the hard work would be for nothing."

Blake nodded his head and stood up out of his chair. He went to the door, opened it, and said, "You know, you are precisely right! My apologies for pressing the issue. You are one smart kid and doing a wonderful job. Keep up the good work. You will make it far in life with your mentality." Then he exited my office.

"Shit," I mumbled.

I was still in shock at how much money Blake had in his pocket, let alone the package was his winnings. Maybe it might be a good thing if I started going with him. I could get ahead of bills; I can buy Karina something nice. A new vehicle, another house, or even take us out to eat at a nice restaurant.

No, you can't think like this, Will. I need to have some common sense; I need to come back to reality. I don't know about sports to make that kind of money. Do you think the boss knows sports like that?

As I am lost in thought, I get a knock on the glass of my office. The same couple that was looking at the luxury vehicle came back. I greeted them with a smile and started to talk to them. They bought the vehicle, so that makes six vehicles sold today. It matches my total from yesterday, which is good.

As the day ended, Blake said, "Since you opened the dealership, I'll do the favor in closing it tonight. Why don't you head home?"

I replied, "Thank you, I'll get my paperwork done and head out.

Once I finished everything, I sat in my vehicle to reminisce about the day.

Then I started driving off, but I drove in a different direction than home. I got on the highway and headed toward Las Vegas.

Once I got there, I headed for the coffee shop I stopped at when visiting the dealership. Instead of going into the dealership, I went into the building that said, 'Place Your Bets Here.' I grabbed the door handle, took a deep breath, and pulled the door open. As I entered, I heard many people yelling. I wonder why they are screaming.

I looked at a group of people yelling at a TV on the wall, and I walked over to them to see what they were watching. It was a sport of some kind; I don't know that game well enough to say which sport it is.

Some guy turned to me and said, "I knew I shouldn't have betted on them. I knew better, but it looks like I'm just donating my money."

"What are you guys doing in here," I said. "This is my first time here, and I don't know anything about sports or betting, but I was interested in coming into this place."

A different guy looked at me and laughed in my face. "You don't know nothing about betting, sports, or any of this stuff?" the guy asked. He grabbed his chin and continued, "Well, come back tomorrow morning, and I will help you; I can give you some advice and tips. One thing I will say, though. You may think you know the teams you choose, but it's more of having luck on your side."

"I don't know if I want to get involved in this stuff, and I was just curious about what all goes on inside here."

"I will tell you; curiosity killed the cat. How about this, if I see you in the morning then good. If not, I know you are strong-willed, more than many of these people who come here."

I nodded my head and left the place.

On the way home, I was thinking about the what-ifs on betting, not telling Karina, winning, losing, and Ashley. When I pulled into the driveway, the sun was already going down. I opened the door to the house, and there was no presence of Ashley waiting for me like she usually does. I placed my coat on the hooks and closed the door behind me.

"I'm home!" I called out.

Karina replied, "Your food is in the dining room. Come sit down and eat."

I walked over and sat down. "Dinner looks amazing, babe."

Karina smiled and gazed at me, "Thank you." There was a pause after that, then she continued, "How was your day, honey? You didn't return my call; I take it you were busy today?"

"Yea, it was quite the day today."

I started telling her about the morning and how it had started.

After I explained, Karina laughed, "That sounds like an eventful day." She placed her elbows on the table, hands under her chin, and continued, "Well, I am glad nothing happened to you. Do you know what was in the package?"

I paused, thought about it for a moment, and said, "No, he was very secretive about the whole thing. I didn't want to press the issue and keep asking questions, so I left it alone."

Did I lie to my girlfriend? We both have been truthful, and I don't want to make a habit of this. Am I the wrong person now for lying to my faithful girlfriend?

Are there secrets maybe she is hiding from me?

"Where is Ashley?" I asked.

Karina replied, "She is in her room. She brought home a book from school, and I helped her read it. After we got done, she wanted to go back and read it on her own."

After dinner, I walked into the kitchen to wash my plate. Karina asked me, "Is everything okay?" She placed her hand on my back and continued, "You are acting a little different today."

I finished washing my plate, placed it in the dish rack, and answered, "I am still stunned at the whole situation that happened today."

"Yeah, it could have gone worse, but you survived. I have the bed made already, so go and see Ashley and get some rest. You have a day off tomorrow; you can sit back and relax."

Chapter 2

woke up from a strange dream in the middle of the night. In my dream, I had walked into the betting place, and Karina was waiting for me inside.

She said, "Is this what you have been doing behind my back?"

Blake walks in and tells me, "Good job, son. You finally took my advice and started making more money on the side."

That is when I woke up. I went into the kitchen and had a glass of water. I sat on the couch to take some deep breaths to help me relax.

Why am I doing this to myself? I never had an urge to want to do something like this so wrong that it is making me do some atrocious things. I had never lied to Karina; I had never hidden anything from her.

Why now? What is making me do these things I could never see myself doing?

I finally shook off the feeling and made my way back to bed. I lay in bed, turned over on my side next to Karina, and held her. She had woken up and knew something was wrong.

Instead of asking about it, she turned to face me, put her head on my chest, and said, "I love you."

As I held her, I kissed her on her forehead, hugged her tighter, and said, "I love you too." Then we both fell back to sleep.

I woke up again, but this time to a ray of bright sunshine in my eyes. As I rolled over to my side, I noticed Karina wasn't there. "Well, good morning, sleeping beauty. Do you want any breakfast?" Karina said from the doorway. I turned onto my back and nodded my head.

The smell of bacon cooking and coffee brewing in the kitchen lifted me out of bed. I splashed some water on my face to help me wake up. I took a long gaze in the mirror as I looked into my eyes. I took a deep breath and thought, this isn't who I am. I honestly do not recognize myself, and my thoughts are not the same either.

I went to the kitchen and saw Karina at the stove with her back turned to me. I walked up to her, put my hands on her hips, and gently kissed her neck.

"You just gave me the chills and goosebumps," Karina said as she shivered.

"So, what is on the agenda for today?"

"Well, my friend wants to come and get Ashley and me for a playdate with her and her daughter. I figured this would be a good time for you to sit back and relax." She then wrapped her arms around me and held me tight.

Karina pressed her head onto my chest and continued, "Maybe when we get back, we could go to the park and spend time together."

"Okay, that sounds like a plan."

Karina and Ashley left, and I was alone, sitting on the couch watching tv. I was flicking through the channels, but nothing caught my interest. In the back of my mind was an image of the betting place, and I shook my head.

No, damnit, Will, get it out of your head. Again, I shook my head no. I could not win against my mind. Why don't I have any control over it? Let's go out there and see what the guy was saying. It won't hurt anything, and I will be back by the time the girls return.

I got dressed, grabbed my keys, and started heading out. In my head, I was thinking it was a bad idea but also thinking it was a good idea. I weighed the pros and cons as if I knew what I was doing. I pulled up to the place, parked the car, and went inside.

As I opened the door, the guy from yesterday noticed me and ran over to me. "Ha! I knew you would show up again." The guy said. "The cat survived the curiosity and felt satisfaction afterward."

I shook his hand and said, "I don't have much time. Can you help me learn what I have to do here?"

"Of course."

The guy gave me the slip with names that looked like they could be sports teams, which I do not know about. He started with the top of the list and went down to the bottom of who they are, where they are, and what type of sport it is. Then he tried to tell me about how a parlay works.

The guy said, "If you select multiple bets from different events and combine them, you could increase your winnings. The catch is that you must win each bet to receive that payout. If you place a bet on three different teams but only two of the three wins, you lose."

"Those odds suck! I could get my hopes up seeing two teams win, but the third team loses, and then I lose."

"That is the name of the game, my good sir."

After the guy gave me everything I needed, I left the place and headed home. I probably spent at least over 2 hours in there. I haven't received a call from Karina, so I should be clear.

During my drive back, I gave Blake a call, and it rang a couple of times and went to voicemail. I left him a voicemail to call me back, or I will talk to him tomorrow at the dealership.

I got home, and Karina still wasn't home yet. I settled in the house, sat on the couch, and took a deep breath to relax my mind and body. That was a lot of knowledge to take in with betting. My mind felt exhausted just from hearing the guy talk. His advice, the do's and don'ts, was a lot to remember. From thinking so much, I created a headache for myself that hurt bad.

As I'm sitting there, I hear the door starting to open. "Daddy! Daddy! Daddy!" Ashley shouted out. She ran to me and showed me a couple of stuffed teddy bears and gifts. "We went to a fair, and these are the things mom and I won," Ashley explained.

I saw Karina walking through the living room. She came over to me and sat next to me on the couch. The look on her face and the noise she made as she sat down sounded like all her energy was depleted.

I asked Karina, "Sounds like you had a lot of fun, huh?"

She laughed and shook her head no.

"Instead of me cooking, how about we order a pizza," Karina suggested as she leaned over to wrap her arms around me.

"Sounds like a plan to me."

Ashley heard pizza and started running in circles, shouting, "Pizza! Pizza! Pizzaaaa! I love pizza!"

After dinner, we cleaned up, and I got Ashley ready for bed. I tucked her in, kissed her forehead, and said, "Good night, princess."

"Good night, daddy."

I left the room and closed the door. I headed for the bedroom and noticed Karina was already all comfortable in bed. I let out a small chuckle as I stood in the doorway.

"What's so funny?!" Karina exclaimed.

"I didn't think you would be in bed already."

"Yea, yea, yea."

I turned off the lights, got in bed, kissed Karina, and said, "Good night."

Karina turned towards me and held me tight. "Good night."

The following day when I got to work, Blake saw me and said, "Hey, I apologize I didn't call you back."

I replied, "It is okay. I wanted to ask you something, sir. It is about the sports bets; I went to this betting building in Vegas yesterday and--."

Blake stopped me before I could finish the rest of my sentence. "That place is not a good place to go. Today, let's close the dealership a little early. I'll take you to the casino where I place my bets, and it is easier and safer than that place."

I agreed and nodded my head.

As the day went by, I thought, is this the right thing to do? Karina told me that we don't have much money to throw around, especially on gambling casually. If I won, would she be mad because we have more money?

I cleaned the showroom, emptied the trash, and wiped down the vehicles. Blake comes up to me and says, "Well, I just about have everything done. Let's head out when you're all set with what you're doing."

"Okay, I'm ready."

"We will head to Vegas. Do you want to ride with me or follow?"

"I'll ride with."

We got to Vegas and pulled up to this vast casino. The building was enormous, and the lights were so bright it was hard to look at. We parked by the doors and had the valet park our car. In the corner of my eye, I had seen Blake slip the valet driver a $100 bill before he got in.

"Is that how much it costs to pay for valet service?" I asked.

Blake answered, "No, it is just being courteous. Giving them tips for their work and how much you give them brings respect. You give them a small or low tip, and they may see it as insulting."

"Just like tipping at a restaurant, right?"

"Something like that, same concept but different in a way."

We entered the casino, and many friendly people immediately greeted us. As we got past the entrance lobby, I heard someone to my right say, "Mr. Fenn, welcome back, sir."

That voice sounds so familiar. I know I had heard it from somewhere but from where? The lightbulb above my head turned on, and I knew where I had remembered that voice. That was the man outside the dealership waiting by the door. He sure looks a lot different as he has a clean tux and shiny dress shoes. Cuff links shined bright as the lights hit them. His dress pants look freshly pressed with no creases whatsoever.

The man turns to me and says, "Hey, no hard feelings from the other day, right? I was tasked to ensure that package was safely dropped off to the right person."

"No, it is okay. I understand that you have a job to do," I replied.

"Good, and welcome to Big Stakes Casino!"

We weaved through all the people and made our way to the bar.

"Do you drink?" Blake asked me.

"No, I don't like the taste of alcohol," I replied.

Blake looked at me, laughed, and said, "Son, I'm going to get you something weak right now. You're with me today, so you're going to have some fun."

I took a sip of my drink, let the flavors marinate onto my taste buds, and swallowed. "This is not bad; I like this drink. What is it called?"

"Tequila sunrise! Don't have too many of those. They will sneak up behind you like a monster in the dark."

We grabbed our drinks and headed for an area with at least 20 colossal tv screens. Each with different sports playing, another tv had a screen that said available bets. It was all a foreign language to me. Even after getting help from the man at the betting place, I couldn't understand what was happening. I had a look like a lost child in a big building.

Blake looks over at me and says, "You ready to start learning how to place sports bets? Do you have a favorite sport that you want to follow when betting?

I start losing my mind after being overwhelmed. I start thinking of Karina right away. I did a bad thing; I will come home smelling like alcohol and wasting money at the casino. I don't know if I should commit to this.

"Hey, is anybody home?" Blake waves his hand in my face as I'm lost in thought.

"This was a bad idea, sir; let's leave."

He looks at me, puts his hand on his forehead, and shakes his head.

"I brought you out here so you can change your mind, huh? No, we are out here and will not return and head home. Let me show you what to do right, and you can fully understand what you're doing."

I nodded my head; then we went to the seating area. He showed me the screen with the betting table. He talked about spreads, the money line, over/under bets, alternative spread bets, and many other placement bets.

"Parlays are your big money winners." Blake explained.

He helped me pick out a three-bet parlay. If I put $50 on this bet with a +596 odds, I could win almost $350. Then another anxiety attack kicked in. I am wasting this money on stuff I know nothing about, and I trust my boss to direct me the right way. What if I lose? That money is gone, down the drain. What am I going to tell Karina?

"Thank you for showing me all of this. I don't know if I can go forward with this, though. I don't think I can afford to lose the money I work so hard for and support my family."

Again, Blake puts his hand on his forehead and shakes it. "You are making this harder on yourself, Will. Look, you wanted me to bring you out all this way for nothing. I have no choice but to do this. If this is how you act whenever you want me to bring you out here, then I won't do it anymore! If you want to be employed at my dealership, let's place this bet, and then we can be on our way."

I sat there with a blank face. I initiated this situation, and now it has turned into something drastic like this. What am

I to do? I need my job, but I don't want to ruin my relationship with Karina.

"Fine, let's place this bet, but this is going to be the only bet I do. I can't afford to lose the only earnings I have coming in to feed my family."

"Okay, that is very understandable. Let me tell you, though, $350 isn't much to make a profit out of."

He showed me some other things I could do on my bets. Once I entered all my wagers, it totaled $5,050. My return would be over $20,000 if all my picks were to win. We headed up to the counter to hand in my slip. Then we left the casino and had the valet bring our vehicle up.

On our way home, I said to Blake, "Hey, I'm sorry for everything back there. The only thing I could think of was my family and what could happen if I didn't win."

Blake smiled and laughed. "You know I was once like you; I was scared that the world would come crumbling down on me over a decision I made. I was scared that if I decided the wrong way on a choice, the world would criticize me for what I did and how I did it. This is your life that you're living, and you only get to live it once."

"Yeah, you're right."

We made it back to the dealership. I shook Blake's hand and said, "Thank you, sir."

"No problem, I will see you tomorrow."

I got into my vehicle, turned it on, and headed home. On the way home, I didn't feel guilty that I had just made this decision. The boss was right, and maybe I needed this in my life.

I pulled into the driveway and headed inside. As I opened the door, Ashley came running to me. "Daddy! Daddy! Daddy!" she yelled. I hugged her, lifted her, and spun her around. As I twirled her, she screamed, "WEEEEEE!!!

As always, I walked into the kitchen where Karina was cooking food. Put my hands on her hip and whispered into her ear, "Hey there, beautiful." She didn't flinch or didn't acknowledge I was there. Nor did she turn around and hit me with a potholder.

"Is everything alright with you?" Karina asked. "You smell like alcohol, and you never drank before. You didn't even call me back after I called you five times!"

My phone was in Blake's car, which is why I never heard it, I thought. Oh man, I'm in deep shit now.

"I'm sorry, babe. We closed the dealership early, and Blake wanted to celebrate a great month we had, so he wanted to go out for some drinks. I told him I don't drink, so he had me try a drink that wasn't too strong from what he told me."

Karina stopped stirring a pot on the stove filled with macaroni and cheese. "You still could have called me back while heading home. Plus, you were driving a little intoxicated also. What if something were to happen to you? I wouldn't have known what was going on!"

"I am sorry I didn't call you back. Yes, I was a little buzzed, but I was fine. I also didn't want to call because I wanted to focus on the road and get home safe."

Karina turned around, hugged me, and started crying. "Please call me next time before attempting something like this again." I nodded my head, kissed Karina, and hugged her tight.

"I love you, buttercup," I said.

"Oh my gosh," she replied as she hit me with the potholder again. Karina amusingly said, "You're a dork. I love you too."

We ate dinner, and I helped her with the dishes. The night grew late, and it was time to put Ashely to sleep. She went to lay down; we both tucked her in and said goodnight.

After we left Ashley's room, we both laid down in bed. Karina got closer to me as I cuddled with her. I held her tight as if I would never let her go. Her back was towards me, and she pulled my head towards her neck. I kissed it ever so gently; the mood felt great. She grabbed my hand and placed it on her breast. I caressed them as I kept kissing her neck. She then turned over and kissed me on the lips. Another everlasting moment and night with Karina.

Meanwhile, at Blake's house:

Blake received a phone call late in the night. The person on the other side of the phone asked, "Is that the guy you were telling me about?"

Blake answered, "Yes, he's the one."

"Are you sure about this? It would be best if you weren't wrong and something happens to you. I have my ways of making incidents or accidents disappear as if nothing happened."

Blake had a startled look on his face, and he swallowed hard. "Yes, I know what you are capable of. I had witnessed it firsthand a couple of times and understand the consequences."

"Good, I am glad we both have an understanding then."

"Do you want me to tell him anything, or will you arrange--."

"No, I will arrange for us to meet together soon."

"Okay."

"Have a goodnight, Fen."

Then hung up the phone. Blake had a worried look as he put the phone down. He stepped outside to light a cigarette, but from the trembling of his hand, it was a challenging task to do.

Blake looked up into the sky as he took his last puff from the cigarette. Then flicked it out into the grass and headed inside.

Chapter 3

One day went by after visiting the casino. I haven't heard anything about if I won anything or not. I got ready for work and headed to the dealership. I got to work and saw Blake sitting in his office. Knocked on the door and said, "Good morning, sir. Have you heard anything about my bets that we had placed?"

Blake responded, "Actually, there is a game on tonight. You should take some time to watch it."

"I'll see if I can. Usually, when I get home from work, I spend time with Karina and Ashley. If I changed anything, she'd know something is going on."

"Okay, that's fine, I understand."

After our conversation, I started walking out of his office and heard Blake say, "You know what you need is another night out to loosen up and relax."

I laughed and replied, "I'll think about it."

Time flew by, and I had closed the dealership for the night. I headed home and got another warm welcome from Ashley and Karina.

During dinner, I got a message from Blake:

> *That game is on right now if you are interested in watching it.*

Karina saw me reaching for my phone and asked, "Who is that?"

I responded, "Just Blake letting me know the numbers for today. We had a great day at the Vegas store."

In my head, I'm still asking myself, why am I doing this? Why am I lying to the love of my life like this? Who have I become?

Karina and I laid down in bed after dinner and tucked in Ashley. Her back was towards me and then turned over, facing me.

"Is everything okay?" Karina asked. "You seem a little off lately?"

I took a deep breath and answered, "Well, lately, I have been stressed at work."

"Oh really? What has been stressing you at work?"

"I want to do my best for Blake and sell as much as possible. These next few months will be our busy times, and I know if we don't do our best, our customers will go to our competitors."

Karina placed her hand on the side of my head and started caressing me. "In my eyes, you will always be #1. You are a very hard worker at home, and I know you do the same at work."

I placed my hand over Karina's and smiled.

The following day, I sat at my desk looking over some paperwork. In my head, I was still asking myself, why am I doing this to her? Karina doesn't deserve this from me.

Blake slammed his hand down on my desk. As I was still thinking in my head, I jumped and returned to reality.

"You look like you're in outer space right now," Blake says.

He closed my door, pulled a chair to my desk, and continued, "What's on your mind? And don't say nothing because I know that look, and it usually spells out danger!"

I paused and sighed, "I haven't told Karina about putting some money down on gambling. I don't know if I want to tell her because I know she will be mad. If I don't tell her and she finds out, it will be worse than if I told her what I did. I don't know what to do. I keep asking myself, why am I doing this?"

Blake looks at me and nods his head. "That is something you must figure out on your own. The best advice I can give you is to do what your gut tells you, and I can help you hide it by going to the casino and making your bets for you."

I look at Blake with a blank face.

"Don't worry, son, I have your back," Blake said. "You keep selling cars for me, and I will ensure everything works out for you in the long run."

He then gets up from his chair, pushes it back to the wall, and walks towards the door. He opens it slightly and says, "Don't worry, I got you covered. Just worry about the sales, and I'll do the rest."

Blake walks out of my office with a big smile and starts talking to a couple looking at a display car in the showroom.

I thought, am I doing the right thing by letting the boss take this over? You know what, Will, don't let it stress you out. It's all going to work itself out in the end.

I got up from my chair and made my way out of the office. I was walking to the middle of the showroom when I received a phone call from Karina. I looked around for Blake; he was still talking to the same couple. So, I stepped outside to take the call.

"Hey, babe," I answered.

Karina had fear in her voice when she said, "Hey, some guy came to the house just now in an all-black outfit asking for you. I told him you were at work, but I could help if he needed anything. He shook his head no and walked away without saying anything. Is everything alright? Is there something I need to know?"

I started thinking to myself, what am I going to say? How am I going to say what's going on? If I tell her, it'll mess up Blake's plans to help me out. What do I do?

My palms started becoming sweaty and sticky. I can feel wet marks forming on my shirt under my armpits. I began to say something, but my voice was scratchy, and I couldn't get a word out.

I tried again to get a word out to say something, so she didn't worry.

As I was about to answer, I coughed and said, "There's--
."

Before I could get another word out, Blake came up behind me and yelled, "Will I need you to get back into the showroom. Some customers were asking for you by name. How great is that, huh?"

"Okay, let me finish with Karina first, and then I will head in."

Blake grabbed the phone from my hand and firmly said, "These opportunities only come by a handful of times. It would be best if you jumped on this right away, and I will talk with Karina until you get back."

I grabbed the phone back and asked Karina, "Hey can you talk with Blake, or do you want to call me back later, and we can finish this?"

She replied frustratedly, "I'll stay on the phone until you get back."

I took a deep gulp and handed the phone back over to Blake. I started walking back into the dealership, but I turned to look back at Blake before entering. He was smiling and laughing while talking on the phone. I thought to myself; maybe this will work out in my favor.

As I walked into the dealership, I noticed there was a very handsome gentleman in a nice suit and tie. It looked like his pants were just freshly pressed. A three-button coat and dress shoes shone brightly when the sun hit them just right.

Next to him is a gorgeous lady in a long red dress that almost touched the floor. Big, flashy diamond hoops hung from her ears.

At first, I thought Blake was only pulling my leg by saying these people were here to get me off the phone. But now that I see them, he was telling the truth. The sweaty, sticky palms returned as I was nervous about approaching them.

The gentleman started walking my way. I started telling myself, alright, Will, get your act together. Stand up straight, and focus.

The gentleman stuck his hand out for a handshake and said with a light Italian accent, "You must be the infamous Will that I keep hearing about. My name is Carlo, and this beautiful lady is Evelyn."

These sound like some influential names; I wonder who they are? Are they here to buy a vehicle? If they're looking for something fancy, we don't have anything in our inventory right now.

I glanced over at Evelyn as she stood there. Everything was beautiful about her. From the way that she smiled to the way that she waved when Carlo introduced her. She had these long sexy legs that protruded from her dress. You could smell the perfume that she was wearing from where I was standing. The fragrance was so pleasant that one whiff and you could start floating in the air towards her. The only thing I could do was stand there and gaze at her. Wait a minute, Will! You love Karina and don't need to be staring at other women like this. I am not a cheater or plan to cheat on Karina.

As I was gazing, Evelyn said seductively, "Careful, leave that tongue out long enough and I might snatch it up."

I returned to reality and turned my attention to Carlo, shook his hand, and said with a smile, "It is a pleasure to meet the both of you. Welcome; how may I assist you today?"

Carlo responded, "Do you have an office we can talk to more privately?"

I was stunned; I didn't know what the real reason for their appearance here was for now. I started telling myself, okay, Will, think wise and focus.

"Yes, I do right over here. Follow me, please."

Carlo nods and tells Evelyn with a smile and a wink, "Stay right here, don't go anywhere."

We both entered my office and sat down. I asked, "So, what brings you over here? What may I assist you with?"

With a big grin, Carlo looked over to where Evelyn was sitting and said, "She's a beauty, isn't she?"

I looked over at Evelyn and then back at Carlo. "I'm sorry, excuse me. I am in an excellent relationship with a gorgeous lady."

Carlo laughs, "Fenn tells me you are a brilliant guy, good with the smooth-talking since you are a salesman, am I right? He also said you have quite the tenacity and diligence."

The name Fenn caught me off guard. Where did I hear that from? It feels so recently that I heard someone call out that name. Then my memory backtracks, and the moment at the casino reappears. That man at the entrance called him that when he welcomed us. So maybe this guy is from the casino.

I sat back in my chair, "Yes, you are right about the smooth talker. So, which of my fine vehicles will we get you into tonight? Maybe, a nice luxury sedan for you and the misses, or how about a sports vehicle with some speed?"

Carlo looks at me with a serious face and then lets a loud comical laugh. "Oh no, you have it all wrong here. I am not here to enlarge my repertoire of fancy carriages, Will. I am here to recruit someone with your skill, with your cunning expertise of knowledge. I am trying to widen my operations and bring you alongside me to help me seize things I can't acquire on my own."

I was stumped for words. Who is this guy? This guy's range of vocabulary far exceeded that of my own. Why does he need me by his side if he is a better talker than me?

I looked at Carlo, confused, "And what do your operations include? What is it that you do for a living if you don't mind me asking?"

"I am the owner of Big Stakes Casino, but I will tell you how it is. I do more than just run a casino, you see. I own a couple of nightclubs also. Evelyn is a manager for one of them and keeps my girls in a straight line. I also run small operations that bring in money on the side to help advance my progress in becoming a successful businessman. I want you to help me lead those operations and bring success to my name. You will conduct the operations as my right-hand man."

As I was about to answer, a man knocked on my office door and let himself in. He is the same man that was at the entrance of the casino. He had a vast envelope in his hand. The man walks over to Carlo and whispers something to him as he hands him the envelope. After the exchange, he walks out and shuts the door behind him.

Carlo takes the envelope and slams it down in front of me. "This is your winnings from what you betted on. That guy went to your place looking for you, but some lady answered, and she was confused about his appearance." Carlo leaned forward and continued, "Let me ask you, does she know what you have been doing with the gambling?"

"No, she doesn't know a thing right now, but eventually, I need to tell her."

"Tsk, tsk, tsk, hmm, that isn't healthy for any relationship to hide things from your partner. She must not be a good companion for you to lie and hide things from her; it would be sad if something were to slip out about what you are doing behind her back."

"Who the hell are you to bring her into our conversation?! Keep her out of this, and why are you talking so ill about her? She is an amazing girlfriend, the love of my life. I need you to leave right now!"

Carlo sits back and smiles. "That's what I need to see. I want to see that side of you released! Let me see that inner Will's appearance that has been held back."

"Get out!"

Carlo gets out of his seat very gently, looks at me, smiles, and then looks at where Evelyn is standing. "Why don't you dwell on the idea for, let's say, a couple of days? We will entertain the subject again when our heads are clear and emotions are gone into the wind."

Carlo walked out of my office and over to where Evelyn was. He put his arm out for her to grab onto it, and they both walked out of the dealership. They entered their vehicle and drove off.

A conversation between Carlo and Evelyn happened in the vehicle as they took off:

Evelyn told Carlo, "I like him; he's cute." Evelyn then started twirling her hair around with her finger and continued, "I would love to get my hands on him."

"Don't worry, beautiful; he will be all yours soon enough."

Evelyn closed her eyes and slowly licked her lips. "Good, I can't wait."

Back at the dealership:

I sat back down in my chair, still enraged by our conversation. I started thinking, what have I started and what have I done?

A slight knock on my door triggered some PTSD emotion inside me as I almost threw a glass plaque on the desk.

Blake walked in, seeing I was infuriated, and said, "I'll leave you alone, but here is your phone. I talked to Karina, and she understood the situation with the mysterious guy coming by."

"What did you tell her?"

Blake shrugged his shoulders, "Well…. I was able to calm her down some. I told her that it was a prank some of the other dealerships were playing on some of us. It just so happened that he wasn't home at that time, and you had to be the one to answer the door. I told her not to be mad at you, and I will deal with this problem."

I sat back in my chair and released a sigh. "Do you know what Carlo asked me?"

"Yes, and did you accept?"

I shook my head in frustration, "You didn't care to tell me any of this ahead of time?! You know Karina's name came out of his mouth in ill fashion. And now he threatened to leak out information to her if I don't accept."

"He is a straightforward man. I do apologize that I didn't tell you sooner. I believe this is a once-in-a-lifetime opportunity that Carlo laid out on the table for you; you should give it some time and think, then accept it."

I went quiet as I started to think of what could happen if I were to accept.

Blake continued, "Don't think of the negatives here. It will not do you any justice thinking of what could go wrong, and you need to think about what can go right."

"How do I tell Karina that I won't be working at the dealership anymore. She would surely think something is up and start questioning things."

"I told you, don't worry about that stuff. I have your back, and everything will be okay."

I nodded my head to agree with Blake.

Chapter 4

One day has passed since I was approached with the offer from Carlo. Many things were on my mind at this point. My family, my job, my success in life, and my future were the essential things chewing away at my brain inside. The question that kept trolling through my mind was, who am I? There was no possible way that I was going to conjure an answer to that question each time it passed through. I had created a new person or a monster that I didn't recognize even when I looked in the mirror.

As I was lying in bed still, I turned to my side. I looked to the window, and the daylight was starting to make its way through the curtains.

I turned my attention to the family photo on our nightstand. Look how happy we are. There is no lying in this photo, no hiding things. I looked at Karina's eyes in the picture and told myself, don't worry, babe. I'm doing my best to figure out what I must do to keep us going.

I rolled onto my other side to a sleeping Karina. Just lying there, innocent, and doesn't deserve someone hiding something that shouldn't be hidden. Love should be overflowing through our pores with honesty and trust. It isn't here, though; the friendship that is the foundation of the relationship is non-existent.

I finally got out of bed, jumped in the shower, brushed my teeth, and refreshed myself for the day to start. I dressed for work, kissed Karina's forehead, and headed to work.

The image of Carlo talking to me was playing on repeat. Each time it replayed, it seemed like the picture got more robust and intense. I could feel his emotion and dedication to recruiting me. There were times that the image would freeze to Carlo with a smug smirk on his face.

As I got to work, I remember Blake telling me, "Can you open the dealership for me tomorrow as I will be late coming in to work."

I got out of the car, opened the dealership, and sat in my office. Sitting there, I told myself I needed to stop thinking about this situation.

I shrugged my shoulders, took a deep breath, and got out of my chair.

I went to the lobby and started making a pot of coffee. Maybe the smell of fresh beans getting roasted will help change the flow of my mood today.

From a distance, I hear the door chime from the door opening. I turned around, and my first customer for the day walked in. I told myself I felt better already.

Half the day went by, and I hadn't seen any sign from Blake. I thought to myself, should I call him? Maybe he's busy, so I'll leave him alone and wait.

I still haven't heard anything from the boss at the end of the day. Now I started to get worried.

I picked up my phone to call him, and nope, right to voicemail. I hope everything is alright. I will give it some time; then, I'll try again.

After forty-five minutes, I tried again, and nothing; it went straight to voicemail again. This is strange for Blake not to contact me all day if he isn't going to show up.

I closed the dealership, turned off the lights, and headed home. I entered the house, and Ashley was there to greet me. I hear Karina from the kitchen, "Welcome home, babe."

As I walked closer to the kitchen, the aroma of garlic, shrimp, and salmon was a refreshing smell to come home to. I walked up behind Karina as she was still cooking, put my hands around her waist, kissed her neck, and told her, "That looks and smells amazing!"

Karina relaxed and rested her body on mine as she stirred the food.

"How was work?" Karina asked.

"It turned out pretty good. The only thing that's worrying me is Blake never showed up. He told me he would be late yesterday, but that's it. I tried calling him, but it went straight to voicemail."

Before Karina could get a word out, I got a phone call. I pulled my phone out of my pocket to see who it was, and Blake was calling me. "Speak of the devil."

I answered, "Hello."

Blake replied, "Sorry to bother you late and for not showing up. I hope it wasn't too much of a hassle."

"No, it wasn't too much of a hassle."

"Good, is it a good time for you to talk? I need you to come to the dealership as soon as possible."

"Can it wait until after dinner? Karina just prepared an amazing meal that smells wonderful."

"I don't think it can wait. But if it must, make sure you come right after dinner!" then hung up the phone.

Karina overheard me and said, "I'll save you a plate. Go ahead and make sure everything is good."

As Karina said that I stood there thinking, what could be happening? Does this involve Carlo? The casino?

"Babe, are you alright?" I hear Karina ask.

I shook my head so that I could focus on Karina.

"Yeah!" I replied. "I will be right back."

I kissed Karina, grabbed my coat, and headed to the dealership. On my way to the dealership, I received another call from Blake.

"Are you on your way?" Blake asked.

"Yes, I should be there in a little bit. Is everything alright? Usually, you don't call me out to the dealership this late at night."

"I will tell you everything when you get here."

I arrived at the dealership. The lights were off inside, but I saw Blake's vehicle off to the side, and I parked by his car and got out.

"What's going on?" I asked.

"It has been a day now, going to be two days. Do you have an answer for Carlo?"

I shook my head and thought I knew it was about that. I didn't even think about an answer or how I would treat the situation, so it didn't mess up my relationship at home. What will Carlo do to me, my family, or Blake if I don't answer today?

"No, I don't have an answer yet. I didn't have a chance to think about it as I thought I would have a couple more days."

Blake hung his head down, turned around, and headed for the entrance to the dealership. In my head, I thought that it couldn't be good.

Blake turned towards me and asked, "Do you know what Carlo is capable of?"

"No, If "you" wouldn't have brought Carlo here, this situation wouldn't be happening."

"What do you mean by "ME"?"

"Yes, You! I was happy and content with how my life was going, and now I am fighting to keep my head above water, hiding this from Karina."

"Who was the one that came to me with questions about gambling? I saw in your eyes that you were serious about it too. Am I lying?"

I didn't have anything to say to that. I kept quiet for a moment, then told Blake, "This decision is messing up my life. The least you could have done was try to talk me out of it. You took it upon your selfish decision to bring me along, knowing it was a bad idea. So, what am I supposed to do now? No, don't answer that. The decisions you made to help me have destroyed or are about to destroy me. I will figure this out on my own."

Blake smiled and shrugged his shoulders, "Suit yourself. But don't blame me for what happens next after this. You are bringing this upon yourself without my help."

I turned and walked towards my vehicle and stopped at my car door. I turned towards Blake and asked, "Is Carlo at the Casino right now? Is he waiting for me to go up there?"

Blake shook his head yes.

"I will call him, but I am taking a day off tomorrow to rethink everything."

"That is fine with me. Call me when you are going to come back."

I shook my head, got into my car, and drove off.

I called Karina but no answer. Maybe she's sleeping already.

Then, I called Carlo, and right away, he answered, "Hello! You have reached Carlo; how may I assist you?"

I replied, "Carlo, this is Will."

"I have been waiting for you to call me. Tell me, do you bear good news?"

"I need a couple of days to think about my decision. I can't let Karina know about any of this."

Carlo chuckled, "Don't let a guy like me wait forever. These opportunities only come a dime a dozen in a lifetime, and I want to see you grow and succeed in life. So please consid--."

"Trust me, I am thinking of everything when I'm making my considerations! I will get a hold of you in a couple of days."

I hung up on Carlo before he could say anything else. I took a deep breath and exhaled as I pulled into my driveway. I sat in my car and just laid back on the seat. I shook my head and screamed out, "Aaaaaaargh!"

I walked into the house, and all the lights were off. I said to myself they must be sleeping already. I feel bad she made a good dinner, and I couldn't even enjoy it with them. I walked into the kitchen and noticed everything was cleaned and put away already. I took my plate out of the microwave, wrapped it, and put it into the fridge.

I made my way upstairs and went into Ashley's room, and she was a sleeping angel. I went over to her and kissed Ashley's forehead. I went into my room; Karina was sleeping too, and still shaking my head, I got into his whole situation.

I changed into my night clothes and lay in bed. I kissed Karina on the forehead and fell asleep.

I woke up in the middle of the night but didn't recognize the room. What happened to everything in my room? Dressers, TV, nightstands, everything was gone except the bed. I reached over for Karina, but no one was there. Where is Karina? What is this place?

I got out of bed, looked in the bathroom, and didn't see anything or anyone.

I walked down to Ashley's room and noticed the space was deserted with no Ashley. Where are everything and everyone?

I got halfway downstairs when I saw a light in the living room. I yelled out, "Karina! Is that you?"

No response, but the light was still there. I walked into the living room, and there was a fireplace with a lit fire inside. We don't own a fireplace, I said to myself.

Am I in a dream world? I heard glass hit the floor in the kitchen. I rushed over there and saw nothing. Windows still intact, I turned around, and everything in the kitchen was gone.

I dropped to the floor with my hands over my head, making a small cry.

"Where is everyone at?" I said, crying.

Suddenly, I hear a voice from a distance, "Babe, we are right here!"

I rushed to my feet and started to look for the voice. I yelled out, "I don't see you!"

On the other side of the house, from where I heard the voice, I listened to another voice giggling, "Daddy, come find me!"

It sounded like Ashley's voice. I yelled out, "Ashley! Where are you?"

No response. I went back upstairs into my room. By the window were Karina and Ashley standing next to each other.

Karina was holding Ashley and crying, "How could you do this to us? I thought you loved us! What did we do to deserve this?"

Ashley sobbed, "Dad! Don't leave us, and we need you here with us."

I ran to them to hug Karina, but they vanished in thin air. I went through the window they were standing next to, and I was there free falling screaming out, "Help!"

I landed on my feet, but I was in the dealership now. All the lights were off except for my office; a small desk light was on. I walked towards it but didn't see anyone in there.

I went to turn off the light and heard a voice call out to me, "We need more cars sold. Our business thrives on what you do."

I yelled out, "Blake, is that you? Where are you?"

I started walking around to see if I could find him. No luck, I could not find anyone in the building.

I was again on the floor, crying with my hands over my head. Then I hear another voice coming from the opposite direction. The voice exclaimed, "You know crying isn't good for someone that's going to take over my operation!"

I called out, "Carlo! This is all your fault. I wouldn't be in this predicament if it weren't for you."

I got up from the floor and dashed towards the entrance of the dealership. I went through the doors, and all I hear are laughs coming from both sides. I feel people touching me and laughing, but I don't see anyone.

Still running, I see a bright light, but something hits my foot, and I fall to the ground. That hurt, I thought to myself.

As I lay on the ground, I saw the rain coming down. Instead of tiny drops, a large amount of water pours over me.

I wake up from the dream on the floor, and Karina is over me with a cup of water.

"What was that for?" I said to Karina.

"You were not waking up, and from the looks of it, you were having a nightmare. Are you okay?"

Karina grabs my hand and helps me up to my feet. "That sure was some nightmare."

"Who is Carlo? What is his fault?"

I took a deep gulp and thought, was I talking in my sleep? How much of it did I say? What was all said?

Think Will, what do you say to Karina? Is she going to believe what I tell her? This can't be good if this is how she finds everything out. Wait, I got it; I know what to say.

"He is a new business partner for Blake. That is what the boss needed to talk to me about yesterday. He wanted me to meet him, and we had discussed this whole situation. I thought a phone conversation would have sufficed, but they both wanted an in-person meeting."

With a startled look, Karina said, "Oh wow, well, that does sound serious. So, he must not be a good person if you guys are in a predicament already?"

I was even more shocked that came out of me. I almost was caught in my lie from how good it sounded.

"He wants to change many things that will destroy Blake's dream and the work that he has done."

Karina sat me on the bed, then pushed me back to lie down and straddled on top of me. "You must remember that change is good sometimes, allowing us to experience new things and move forward in life. We obtain different perspectives or angles in a diversity of ways. Being open to that change and learning new skills can bring about a transformation you never knew was possible."

The only thing I could think of in my head when Karina said that was wow. It was like she knew what was going on in my head. I was fighting demons that only I could see, but after that, it felt like she could see them too.

"You are exactly right," I replied. "I will give this new change a chance to see where it goes."

I think I just found the answer I was looking for. This opened my eyes to something new and some direction.

I kissed Karina and said, "I love you. Thank you for saying that, and I needed to hear those words to uplift me."

Karina hugged me and looked into my eyes, "I love you too."

Chapter 5

The day after, I called Blake to tell him I was taking an extra day off to do some thinking. I feel good about my decision, but I must ensure this is the smart thing. It's not just me; I also have to think about Karina and Ashley.

I took Karina and Ashley to the park in the middle of the day. The sun was out, and a pleasant slight breeze felt amazing.

I bought a kite so we can try flying it. Again, I'm looking at smiles and laughs coming from both Karina and Ashley. Is this genuinely worth burning all this down? No, you have to be optimistic, Will.

"Daddy, let's run faster!" Ashley yells out to me.

I look over at Karina, and I can see the love in her eyes as she watches us run around.

Ashley yells out to Karina, "Your turn, mommy!"

As Karina gets up from sitting on the ground, I feel my phone vibrating. The number looks familiar, but I don't recognize it. I shrugged my shoulders and ignored the call.

As I put my phone in my pocket, I saw Carlo by a shroud of bushes, smiling and waving. Then he walked away. I had a look of disgust on my face, and Karina's smile turned to a frown as she saw my face.

"What is that face for? And what are you looking at?" Karina Asked.

I knew why he was there, letting me know his eyes were always on my family and me. Scare tactic to try to get me to give him an answer. But how did he know I was at the park of all places.

I returned to reality and saw Karina waving her hand in front of my face.

"Hello! Earth to Will, do you copy?" Karina said.

"Huh."

"I asked you a question, but you never answered!"

"I'm sorry, I thought I had seen someone that came to the dealership a while back and gave us a hard time."

"Oh wow, when did this happen? You never mentioned that to me before."

"No, it happened a while ago, and it must have slipped my mind, and I didn't say anything when I got home."

Karina walked over to Ashley so she could help her with the kite.

I felt another vibration from my phone, but it was a single one this time. I looked, and it was a text message from the same number. It read:

> *I'm still waiting for an answer. You and your family look pleased now; I would hate to spoil that moment.*

I put my phone back into my pocket and focused on my family time.

The next day, I came back to work. I sat down in my office and turned my computer on. I heard a knock on my door and saw it was Blake. He pulled up a chair, stuck his hand out to me for a handshake, and asked, "No hard feelings about the other day, right?"

"Yeah, no hard feelings."

"I know this isn't probably what you want to hear right away, but did you give him an answer yet?"

I let out a big sigh, "No, not yet, but I think I will call him later and tell him my decision."

"Okay, that's all I need to know."

He got out of the chair, walked towards the door, and stopped. He turned my way and said, "I'm glad your back; it's been quiet here with no one to talk to."

I laughed, "Thanks, it feels good to be back in my office."

The day flew by, and it was almost time for the dealership to close. I grabbed my phone and looked at it for a couple of minutes. What do I say to him? I thought to myself. Oh well, might as well get it over with, I said to myself.

I hit the call button, and it rang twice when it was picked up.

"You sure took your sweet time calling me back. I thought I would have to pay the family a special visit," Carlo said.

I replied, "Please, leave my family out of this! I am the one you want, not them. And my answer is yes; I will join you, okay."

"You just put a smile on my face. I guess Christmas came early this year, didn't it?"

"I only have one request. We meet to discuss some things I want while working for you."

"I like a man that knows what he wants. That's why I choose you for the job. How about we meet at my club by the casino? I say in three days you can come after work."

"How bout I take a half-day to come around late afternoon time, and then I'll still make it home for dinner."

"Sounds good to me. I'm glad you choose my side of things. Bye-bye."

I hung up the phone, and at the door was Blake. He immediately had a massive smile, and I already knew what he was thinking.

"I'm glad you gave him an answer," Blake said. "I can get back to my normal life without him pestering me about this whole thing."

"You and me both."

I got home, and Karina had pizza waiting for me on the stove.

"I got our favorite, garlic crust and supreme no mushrooms," Karina said.

I replied, "Thank you, baby. You're the best!"

I went over to her, hugged her, and held on to her.

Concerned, Karina asked, "Is everything alright?"

"Yeah, just glad to be home."

Three days went by, and I talked to Blake about what Carlo and I had planned. He was okay with me taking a half-day to discuss some things.

I started heading out to the club. I had a bad feeling about going to this place alone.

I pulled up to the place, and this club was a gentleman's club. Ocean's Paradise is the name of this place. I surely don't think this is a good idea to go in there.

I walked in, and the man inside asked me for my name. I told him who I was, and he showed me where Carlo was sitting.

The music in the background and the women walking around half-naked. I knew I was in a different atmosphere than I'm used to. I have never been in a gentleman's club before and never knew what it looked like inside. Gorgeous women were walking around casually like it was nothing, rubbing their hands all over my shoulders as I walked past them. The women were climbing metal poles and dancing on them.

The man brought me to Carlo's table. Evelyn and five other women sat around him. The attention he was getting from all these women, drinks that looked expensive were sitting on the table.

"Sit! You're making me nervous just standing there," Carlo said.

I sat down and stared at Carlo as he casually flirted with the other girls around him. He looked over at me and said, "Would you like a drink? It's on the house today, especially the expensive ones."

"No, I am okay."

Carlo softly placed his hand on Evelyn's lap and said, "Do you remember Evelyn?"

She waved her hand and enticingly bit her lip as he reintroduced her.

"Yes, I remember her."

She got up from her seat and sat on my lap. Caressing my chest with both hands and then onto my arms. She stared into my eyes and said seductively, "The things I would do to you." As she said that, she started to bite her bottom lip and kept staring at me.

I turned my attention to Carlo and said, "Why did you bring me here? I have a girlfriend and don't want any of these women; I want to talk business, not to become a cheater and mess with a stripper."

Evelyn grabbed my face and turned it towards her. "You don't know what you are missing, baby. You are working for Carlo now, so all this and more is yours. You say the word, and whatever you desire will happen."

"No, that's not going to happen, sorry."

I turned my attention towards Carlo again and said, "Are we going to talk business or not? If not, I'm goi--."

Evelyn grabbed my face again so that I was looking at her. "Don't you see! This is your business proposition right here. You have me all on you; how about we take this to a private room so we can talk alone? Maybe give you a preview of what could be all yours one day."

Evelyn lifted her finger under my chin and leaned to kiss me. I turned my head as she got close.

"I told you, I'm not here for that kind of stuff."

Carlo looked my way and said, "Fine, let's talk. Evelyn, give us a minute, then he's all yours."

All the girls walked away, and Carlo sat right next to me.

"So, talk!" Carlo said.

"I want my family left out of anything you have going on. They are not to be harmed in any way, shape, or form. It's bad enough that if Karina finds out what I'm doing, she will leave me. I'm not doing a thing with any women, and I love Karina too much to mess with these… these skanks here."

"You love her so much that you're willing to lie to her about what you're doing! That doesn't make much sense to me, and you will need something more to make me believe you still love her as you say you do."

"I said what I said. I don't need to prove to you my love for her. I know how much I love her, and that's all that matters. Now, what will come of my job at the dealership?"

"Well, that is an easy one. Your job will be terminated, and Fenn will need to find a replacement from one of his other stores. Anything else, your highness?"

"What will be my responsibilities for my job?"

"You will conduct particular tasks assigned to you. Being my right hand, you will be considered top tier. So that means prestige and great influence will be your most prominent attributes."

The time rolled by as we conversed about many other things. Then, I stood up and said, "Okay, that is all I had to ask. I will wait for you to call me."

Carlo smiled and rubbed his hands together. "Where are you going? It is still early, and the fun is about to begin."

I had a confused look and was scared of what might happen next. A couple of waiters came around the corner with silver platters and covers over them.

"I ordered steak and lobster for our celebration dinner!" Carlo excitedly said.

"No thank you. Karina is cooking and waiting for me to get home."

As I walked away from the table, I was stopped by Evelyn. She placed her hand on my chest and said, "You're not going anywhere, big boy. I still didn't have my fun with you yet."

"Go find someone else to have your FUN with! I'm not your guy for that."

"Soon enough, I will break you. I will bring down that protective barrier you have going on and expose your true feelings for me. You just watch and see." As Evelyn finished her sentence she gave me an enticing wink.

I walked out of the club and got into my vehicle. What am I getting myself into? I can't go home smelling like this. If Karina found out I was in a strip club, she would be irate. This is bad, really bad. What do I do?

I called Blake, but no answer. Damn, I said to myself.

Maybe I'll contact Karina to tell her I'll be late and then get home when she's asleep. What if she doesn't fall asleep immediately and is still awake when I get home. Oh great, this is just great. I am definitely in deep shit. I guess I'll take my chances and call Karina.

I called Karina, no answer. She can't be sleeping already. I hit my head, trying to think what to do. I'll call and leave a message saying I'll be home late.

What if something is wrong? Maybe Carlo didn't like how I walked away, and he was punishing me by messing with my family. He didn't agree to leave them alone when I demanded it. Oh great, now I'm overthinking.

I decided to head home, hoping I could sneak in without being noticed. I can take a shower, get rid of these clothes, and everything will be okay. I told myself that I had at least an hour's drive before getting home; that's enough time for Karina to call me if she was awake. So many possibilities were running through my head as I passed each mile marker on the highway.

I got home, and all the lights were on. Oh great, I said to myself. What am I going to do now? I thought about just waiting it out; maybe she would fall asleep. What if she's in trouble and I need to get in there? I started hitting my forehead with my palm saying come on, think, think Will. What are you going to do?

There's only one thing to do, and that's to go inside and face this head-on. I took a huge deep breath and exhaled as I opened the car door. I walked to the door, grabbed the knob, slowly turned it, and opened the door. I walked in, and I saw suitcases by the door. What is this about? What is going on?

Karina yells to Ashely, "Do you have all your stuff together?"

What is going on? I closed the door and headed to the room. Karina saw me as I approached the door and started crying.

Before I could get a word out, she belted, "How could you?! I trusted you, yet you go and do something like this! You get involved in something like this and put our family in danger! What else have you been sneaking behind my back about?"

"What are you talking about?"

Karina, pissed off, closed the dresser door behind her hard and walked over to me. She placed her finger into the middle of my chest, "My friend told me everything! She works at the club you visited and saw everything. I can't believe you!"

I took a step back and took a deep gulp. This was it; I didn't want Karina to find out this way. Primarily through a friend that saw her man at a gentleman's club with a female on his lap.

Karina shook her head and let it hang down.

What am I to say? I can't deny it because I knew what I had done. Is sorry going to help this situation or make it worse?

Karina said in an angry tone, "Well, are you going to say anything?!"

I stuttered, "I am sorry; I should have told you what I was do--."

"You can save those apologies for someone that cares to hear them. I am taking Ashley to my friends' house and staying there until you can get your life together. This isn't the Will I fell in love with! Who are you? What possessed you to make these judgement calls and not say anything to me?"

Karina walked by me and used her shoulder to push me out the way. She grabbed Ashley and started walking to the door.

I said, "Karina! Let's talk about this for a second before you go! Let's work this out!"

Karina stopped midway through the door; you can hear her crying with her back turned towards me. She stood there for a couple of seconds and said, "Talk... About... It." She turns towards me and continues, "You should have thought about TALKING before you decided to do this on your own! The consequences of your actions are leaving you lonely right now! You know what, call that girl that was on your lap. Maybe she could keep you company tonight!"

She then turned towards the door, and Ashely cried, "I don't want to leave daddy!"

"Daddy did something bad, honey; you will see him again, okay. We are just going to stay at someone's house for a while, okay."

The door slammed shut after Karina walked through it. I could only stare down the door as if she would return and accept my apology.

What have I done? I kept saying it repeatedly until tears started running down my face. I tried giving Blake a call again, but it went straight to voicemail.

All her stuff was gone, especially Ashely's. Nothing was left; this house felt empty now.

I went to lay down on the bed to take in all of this, and then I heard my phone ringing. I looked over and saw it was Carlo. I answered, "Right now is not a good time."

"There is something I need you to see. Meet me at the dealership."

I looked at the time, and it was past 9 pm. What does Carlo want with me at the dealership?

"Why do you need me over there?"

Carlo laughed, "You will see!" and hung up the phone.

What else can go wrong on this day? I got up, wiped the tears off my face, and headed to the dealership. The only thing that kept replaying in my mind was watching Karina leave and how she shut the door on the way out. It repeatedly played while driving, and I couldn't stop thinking about it.

I got to the dealership, and inside, all the lights were on. This can't be good, I said to myself. I walked into the dealership, and I heard Carlo in the back yelling, "We are back here!"

I walked past the offices into our storage room. This room has everything for cleaning the vehicles and office supplies. At one point, Blake told me that this room was used to house the cars that needed to be verified for services or basic cleaning.

I walked in, and Carlo sat in a chair next to a tied-up Blake, kneeling with duct tape over his mouth. I was shocked when I saw what was going on and Carlo had a gun to Blake's head, smiling.

I yelled out, "What are you doing?"

"Sit!"

I grabbed the chair and was still in shock at the situation. Tears running down Blake's face were hitting the ground. Behind him is Evelyn, with a big smile similar to Carlo's.

Carlo, still smiling, said, "So, let me get this straight; I heard about what happened to your relationship back home. Tsk…. tsk…. tsk, what a shame. Young love was destroyed before our eyes to something that could have been avoided. But that is fine; everything is going according to my plan; I don't know about yours, though."

Evelyn approached me, put her hand on my chest, and started caressing me. Flirtatiously she said, "With her gone, now I can have you all to myself."

She moved closer to try to kiss me, and I turned my head so she would miss. She became irate that I wasn't giving in and slapped me hard. The slap was hard enough that I almost fell out of the chair. Afterward, she walked behind Carlo and placed her hand on his shoulders.

Still holding the gun to Blake's head, Carlo said, "I want to know how serious you are about doing some of the work I give you. I need proof that I won't have any trouble with you."

"What do you need me to do?"

"Funny you ask that. I thought you would cuss me out and tell me you were done. Possibly even walk away from the entire situation. I may need you to get your hands dirty to answer your question. So, I have a test subject for you right here." As Carlo said that he turned his attention to Blake.

I shook my head and said, "No! I will not shoot Blake."

Carlo laughingly said, "No, no, no, you have it all wrong. I don't want you to shoot or kill, but I want you to teach your old boss a lesson. He was trying to get out of my operation without my consent. Now, if it's something you won't do, I'll put a bullet through his head right in front of you. So, what will it be?"

"Give a lesson? Like, beating it into him?"

"Precisely."

I cannot do something like this to Blake. After everything he had done for me, he took me in when I was searching for a job. Why does this day have to be like this?

"I won't do that, but if there is something else you need to be done, I will do it. But I will not attack Blake like that."

Carlo shook his head in disbelief and hung it low. "Well, suit yourself." He cocked the gun back and pointed it closer to Blake's head. Under the tape, you can hear Blake crying for help.

"Stop! Okay, I will do it."

Carlo stopped, smiled, and took a step back. With both hands, he waved to Blake and said to me, "He is all yours then."

I walked toward Blake, and every memory between him and me went through my head. I got up to Blake and cried, "I am sorry, please forgive me."

I balled both my fists up and thought about what I was doing. I reached back to send a punch flying towards Blake until I heard 'BANG.'

I turned my head toward Carlo in shock as he was pointing the gun at Blake. I looked down at Blake, who had a bullet hole from one side of his head to the other. His body fell to the ground and made a thud sound.

My eyes lit up, and feelings started hitting me. I fell to the ground to get Blake, but he was gone already. Holding Blake in my arms, I yelled to Carlo, "Why would you do that? I was going to do what you had asked!"

"You were taking too long, and I have things to do still. If you're going to take this long before throwing a punch, I have some work to do."

I dropped Blake from my arms and was in Carlo's face. Carlo said, "My work here is done, come Evelyn. We have pressing business matters to deal with back at the casino. I'll get ahold of you, Will, when I have a job for you."

Carlo and Evelyn headed for the exit and left.

This is my fault, I thought as I dropped to the floor and gazed at Blake's body. I got up from the floor and heard my phone ring, and it was Carlo.

I answered, and he said, "I need someone to manage the dealership until I can find out what to do with it. You will be that person that runs it. Don't worry; I'll take care of the other dealerships. Just worry about this one. Thanks." Then he hung up the phone.

I sat back down with my back on the wall. I was thinking about what all had happened in one day. I need time to comprehend all of this. I'll head home, get some sleep, and everything will return to normal. No, it won't, Will. What are you thinking? I hit my forehead again with my palm. Tomorrow I'll have a plan; let me go home and get some sleep.

Chapter 6

One month has gone by since I took over the dealership. Since then, Carlo has shut down the other dealerships and relocated the people to different places and the vehicles over to my business. I got the dealership cleaned up and Blake's body taken out.

I kept my office where it was and left his office empty. Of course, each day has gone by, and it is soundly quiet in the dealership. Every day I would hear his laugh throughout the building.

Still no word from Karina or Ashely either.

During this time, I have developed a relationship with Carlo and some of the guys I am working with. Carlo had given me small jobs and sent me across the United States for some projects of his.

Many people have been coming into the dealership asking what happened to the other buildings and where Blake is. Each day I conjure a new lie for every new person asking these questions. I will say this: business has grown since I took over, and the others closed.

At the end of each day, I usually drive out to Big Stakes casino and place wagers on sports. Since I work for him, I can work up a tab and pay it off when I can. It's a nice feature to have, especially for someone that doesn't know his sports, and my winnings aren't as big as when Blake had helped me out.

After leaving the casino, I head home, expecting open arms patiently waiting for me when I get there. I walk through the door to an empty house. It does get depressing, but before she left, Karina did say once I get my life together. So, there is a chance that she might come back, and I'll be able to see Ashley and have my happiness back in my life.

After dinner, I sat down on the couch to relax. My phone started ringing, and it was Carlo.

I answered, "What's up, Carlo?"

Carlo replied, "I need you and the boys to head downtown for an errand. I have a friend that needs some help tending to a problem."

"Tonight?"

"Yeah, tonight before it gets too late."

Then he hung up the phone. I let out a sigh before getting off the couch, and I went to the room, got dressed, and headed for the casino.

As I arrived, his men were waiting for me at the entrance. I switched into their vehicle and took off downtown.

We arrived at a pitch-black building that looked abandoned. I asked the guys, "Are you sure this is the place?"

The driver responded, "This is the address given to me."

We got out of the vehicle and headed into the building. It's empty, I thought to myself, not a soul in sight. The eerie silence and dark scenery occurred to be a little creepy. We got to a door that had lights on the other side.

I knocked on the door, and a sliding window on the door slid open.

"Who are you? What business do you have here?" a man asked from the other side of the door.

I replied, "We were sent here on a business trip to see a man named Francisco."

"Are you Carlo's men?"

"Yes."

The sliding window closed, and the door opened up. The man walked us into a vast room that looked like an underground casino.

A lot of people were here in lovely, fancy suits. Women wore bright, shiny diamonds around their neck, wrist, and on their ears.

This was no original casino; this was something kept away from society and ceased from existence.

The back corner looked like a boxing ring, but no one was sitting around it. Slot machines scattered across the floor and tables that hosted many different games.

The man took us to the office where we met the guy named Francisco. The man left once we were in the office and closed the door behind him.

Francisco said with a Spanish accent, "You guys must be Carlo's men that I had asked for, and you must be Will. Glad to bask in such high presence."

I nodded and said, "What is it you need for us to do, Francisco?"

"Call me Frank, I have a partnership with Carlo, and he's aiding me with his security staff's help. I have a problem, a big problem. A man came in and disrupted the flow of my joint here. He took out a couple of my security personnel and stole some money from me. I need him dealt with."

"Do we have a location on where this guy is at?"

"Yes, I have it right here."

Frank hands me a paper with the name of a place and address. 'Pete's Pawn Shop' is the place this guy is at. It's almost midnight, and I doubt this place is open right now.

I put the paper in my pocket and told Frank, "It's close to midnight, and I don't think the place is open right now. How bout I venture over there tomorrow?"

Frank laughed, "Oh, trust me, it's open still. Maybe not for business, but it is open."

I had a look of confusion about what he meant by that. Something doesn't seem right in my mind, and I feel like I'm getting set up for failure.

We arrived at the pawnshop that Frank told us about, but no lights were on. I got out of the vehicle to take a look around. I looked through the glass window, and I didn't see anyone there. The store was still full of stuff but didn't look like anyone was there.

After some searching around the building, it seemed no one was there. So, we got into our vehicle and discussed what to do next.

As our driver shifted the car to drive, one of the lights inside came on. It became suspicious, so the driver turned off the vehicle, and we waited to see what was happening.

Two men entered the room; one stood behind a counter and the other on the other side of the counter talking. The man behind the counter matched the description that Frank had given us.

After some time had gone by, a lady walked in where they came in from. Before she got up to the counter where the guys were standing, they had rushed to put away whatever they were looking at. She wasn't supposed to know what they had in front of them from how fast they reacted.

Meanwhile, back at the underground casino:

Frank receives a call from Carlo asking, "Any word from my men yet?"

Frank answered, "No, nothing yet. It's been quiet on my end."

"Okay, I have other business to talk to you about. Do you remember Antonio?"

Frank paused for a moment to think. "Isn't that the old man that runs the Enchanted Tomb casino down from yours?"

"Yes, him. From the rumors I heard, he has been sending people to lurk around my casino. I have had problems with him back in the day, and it's looking like he's back for more problems."

"That's one brave old man. Is he trying to take over all of Vegas? Let's hope he doesn't try anything funny."

Carlo laughed, "Yeah, I'll be ready for him this time. Make sure you keep an ear out for his name. I'm sure someone knows his intentions or has information."

"Of course, I will let you know." Carlo then hangs up the phone.

Back at the pawnshop with Will and the others:

An hour had passed, and something was stirring inside the pawnshop. The lady starts yelling at the two guys and pointing at something inside a display case.

The man we are after isn't saying anything, but the other guy is waving a gun around, pointing towards the entrance door. As if he's trying to tell her to leave out of the store.

I got tired of waiting and told the driver, "Stay put; I'm going in through the back door."

I grabbed one of the guys for backup in case something got out of hand. We snuck around to the back, and you can hear the lady yelling at the guys. From the sounds, she's hollering about something she never received.

I told my partner, "We only care about the guy we are after, and I am not too worried about the others unless they put up a fight."

He nodded to agree with me. We slowly opened the door to a dark storage room. It was so dark; you couldn't see anything in front of you. It's good that our phones have a small light on them to help us see. We get to the door that heads into the room where they are at. We need to be smart about this, or else we won't live through this night.

I told my partner, "On the count of three, we will rush in. You get the guy with the gun, and I'll get our guy. Okay, ready? One, two, thr--."

Before I can say three, we hear a gunshot. BANG! We both became frightened. From the other side of the door, you hear a man's voice say, "Why did you do that?"

I cracked open the door to see what was going on. The lady was lying in a puddle of blood. She had been shot, but by who. It must have been by the guy that was waving the gun around.

I told my partner, "Now is the time; let's move as planned!"

We both rushed the door; I grabbed my man, and my partner tackled the other guy. I think I was more shocked than the other guys because it actually worked.

I told the guy I was holding, "You have been causing some problems at a nearby casino, and you will be taught a lesson not to mess with the owner."

I pushed the guy onto the floor and jumped on him before he could wiggle away from me. I started punching him, one right after another. Headshots, once he blocked them, I went for body shots. I kept repeating them after getting through his blocks until he couldn't defend himself.

I got off of him, and the guy tried to speak but was in too much pain. He could get some words out, but they didn't make sense.

Finally, after getting his breath back, the guy said, "That…. wasn't…. me…. that caused…. all of that."

I took a step back and had a look of confusion on my face as he said that. Then I told him, "Why should I believe you?"

As I said that, behind me, I heard a gun cock back. I turned around, and the guy with the gun had taken my partner hostage. He blurted out, "The man you're looking for is me!"

At this point, I didn't know what to do. I put my hand on my pistol but didn't bring it out in case it would startle the guy.

The guy said, "You think you're a badass and can come here like that? You don't know anything. I should drop your partner right now and then drop you right where you stand."

My partner said, "Don't worry about me; just take him out!"

"Shut up!" exclaimed the guy as he hit my partner in the back of the head with his gun. Then the guy picked my partner up from the floor as he held the gun to his head.

The guy asked, "So, what are you planning to do? Be a hero and save your partner? Take me out as I take out your partner, or be a dead man like your partner here? The choice is all yours."

As I started to conjure a plan in my head, I looked out the window behind the guy. The driver and our other partner slowly crept to the entrance door with guns. I thought to myself, maybe this will be in our favor.

The guy shouted, "What are you looking at, fool?! You should be worrying about your partner here. Oh hell with it." Then pulls the trigger and shot my partner in the head. His dead body hits the floor, making a thud sound.

I couldn't believe it; he had just shot my partner. This just turned into a horrible situation. I diverted my eyes from my partner back to the guy, and the gun was pointing toward me now. I didn't have any time to pull mine out now. Any movement, and he would shoot me dead.

The guys from outside busted through the window before I could conjure a plan. They tackled the guy with the gun.

As he hit the floor, his weapon flew out of his hand and over to the door behind me. I walked over to the guy as we rolled him onto his back. I stood over him and started laying punches into him, and I got done, and my fists were covered in blood.

"We need to get out of here!" the driver yelled.

The driver and the other partner ran outside into the vehicle. I stood over the guy, pointing my pistol at him. I said to the guy, "This is for my partner!" Then took the shot, aiming at his head.

From the vehicle, I can hear the driver yelling, "We need to go! Hurry your ass up!"

Without hesitation, I ran outside and into the vehicle. Then we drove off to the underground casino. In my head, all I could see was my partner getting shot. Then, I would see Blake in my head when Carlo shot him.

Too much blood, too much killing. Why did I even accept this offer? I am not cut out for this type of work.

How I miss Karina and Ashley. I wish I could go home and hug both of them right now.

We arrived at the casino, and I told the driver and the other partner, "I can't believe this just happened."

The driver said to me, "This is our line of work. You will experience this and have to learn to live with it. Let's go inside and give our details to Frank."

I rolled out of the vehicle and couldn't barely stand. As some people would say, I was weak in the knees and had to hold on to whatever was next to me to walk forward. We enter the casino and head to the lounge where Frank is sitting.

"There's only three of you," Frank said. "There were four when you came in. Where is the other guy at?"

I replied, "There was a situation that happened. The information about the guy you gave us was for a different person. Our guy was in the pawn shop but with another guy and a lady. I ended up attacking the wrong guy, the one we were after shot our other partner."

Frank paused, and his jaw dropped. "These things aren't supposed to happen like this, my apologies. It is a risky business we are in, though."

Frank signals for one of his workers over to him. Frank then tells him, "Take care of these guys. Whatever they need, food, rest, or booze. I owe them that much."

"I will have to decline the offer. I need time to process what happened tonight, and also, I need to inform Carlo of all details."

I looked to the driver and said, "Let's head back to Big Stakes."

He nodded to agree with me. The three of us got into the vehicle and headed out. We arrived and headed inside to talk to Carlo, and we met him in his office and told him about what happened tonight.

After we told him, Carlo put his hand on his forehead and shook his head in frustration. He said, "This business isn't for the faint of heart. One reason why I chose you to lead this operation. I know you have grit, kid, and can take it. You did well out there."

"Would it be alright if I took a couple of days off and went to see my parents?"

"Absolutely, I can arrange for a plane tomorrow afternoon to take you back home. Then, when you come back, give me a call."

"Thank you, sir."

After the conversation, I left the casino and headed home. I walked in, ran upstairs, and lay in the bed. I stared at the ceiling for a moment that felt like forever.

Images of everything that has happened in my life kept popping up. Blake, Karina, Ashley, the pawn shop incident.

What am I putting myself through? Why am I doing this to myself?

I picked up my phone, scrolled through my contacts, and stopped on Karina's name. Something inside me was telling me to call her. But, simultaneously, it was trying to pull the phone out of my hand. I wanted to tell her I was sorry, ready to change and leave everything behind me.

Maybe moving to a different state or city is good for us. I started to think of life as if all of this had never happened.

Birthday parties, spending days at the beach, even going to the park, enjoying being outdoors away from all this.

My phone slipped out of my hand and hit the bottom of my chin. I came back to reality from my dream world. All this isn't going to happen, I made my bed, and now I got to lay in it.

I got up, brushed my teeth, washed up, and got ready for bed. I turned off all the lights, lay in bed, and fell asleep.

I woke up to the feeling of someone rubbing my arm. My vision was somewhat blurry, but I wiped my eyes at someone standing next to me. A voice called out to me, "Babe, are you going to sleep all day?"

I looked out the window to the bright sun. I finally could see clearly, and it was Karina smiling. I thought to myself, how long did I sleep? I said to Karina, "You're back? When did you come back?"

Karina replied, "What do you mean? I never left silly. I've been waiting for you to wake up so we can enjoy the nice weather."

I paused and stayed quiet with a confused look on my face. I told Karina, "But you left with Ashley the other night, and it's been over a month already since you left."

Karina laughed and said, "You must have been dreaming of it. I have been here this whole time. Come on, get up, and get ready for the day. I'll make some breakfast for you."

Karina leaves the room; I'm still lying in bed, confused. I thought, what is going on? I finally got out of bed and headed for the kitchen. I don't see anyone; the kitchen is empty. The living room was deserted. Karina shows up from the hallway, enters the kitchen, and says, "Oh good, you're finally awake, sleeping beauty. Let's get ready for the day; I got a lot planned for us to do."

I asked Karina, "I thought you were making breakfast?"

Karina laughs and says, "Breakfast? You know it's evening, right?"

I looked outside, and the sun was getting ready to set. I turned back to talk to Karina, and she was gone. I looked around the house again, and no one was there.

I hear a laugh coming from the living room. A man is laughing from the sound of it. I walked over to the living room and saw Blake sitting there. He asked me, "Are you ready to come back to work? You have been off for a week, and I need my #1 salesman to keep my business going."

I stood there with a confused look and heard pans clinging together from the kitchen. I walked into the kitchen to see Karina ready to make a meal. She says to me, "Your home from work early! Was the boss feeling generous today?"

I wanted to break down and cry. What is going on? This must be a dream! I need to wake up; this isn't real. I went back to the bedroom; nothing was in there. No bedroom furniture, nothing; it was a completely empty room.

I turned to walk out of the room, and Karina was right there. She placed her hand on my chest and said, "Ashley is sleeping. You know what that means, right?" She then pushed me back, and I fell to the ground, but I kept falling like I was free-falling from the sky. It felt like I would plummet forever until I hit the ground.

I woke up screaming on the floor in my bedroom in a puddle of sweat. I had a dream; no, I was having a nightmare. But that nightmare felt real. I got up from the floor and went into the kitchen to get a glass of water. I sat down and drank my water to help me relax. I could feel my heart beating like it would come through my chest.

I took two ibuprofens to help my headache and headed back to bed. I lay there still looking at the ceiling, hoping the dream wouldn't come back.

I need to relax and have a clear mind. I pulled the blanket up to cover and let out a long sigh. Tonight has been a rough night, but I need to get some sleep. I turned off the light on my nightstand and went back to sleep.

I woke up and headed to the airport that Carlo told me to go to. I got on the plane and headed home. I didn't have a chance to call my parents to let them know I was coming, so hopefully, they will be home.

The plane landed in St. Paul, and a cab took me to the house.

We arrived, and I looked at how the house looked exactly the same as when I left. I approached the door and knocked a couple of times but didn't hear anything and thought, damnit, I should have called.

As I was going to turn around and walk away, I heard the door opening, and my father was at the door, happy as ever to see me.

My father said, "Welcome home, son. What brings you out here? Where's Karina and Ashley?"

I looked at him and sighed, "That is one of the reasons why I am here."

As he nodded, my father replied, "Well, come in. Your mother went to see your aunt and won't return for a few days. Are you hungry?"

"No, I ate something before getting on the plane." I entered the house and closed the door.

My dad took me to the living room and said, "Sit, take a load off. Tell me everything, son."

I told my dad what had happened in my life up to this point. He looks at me and says, "Will, every man sings his songs differently than the other man. By songs, I mean life. My tune and melody are going to be unlike yours. It works for me, but it may not make sense to you why I did it that way. And things happen for a reason; your consequences result from your actions. Maybe it was fate that it all worked out this way. Don't let it eat you away inside. Everything has a way of coming back around."

Then I told him about Evelyn. He said, "She sounds like a gorgeous lady. Looks aren't everything, Will. She may be beautiful outside, but the inside is where the natural beauty resides."

I replied, "Thank you, Dad, you were always good at giving me advice. I'm glad I got to come out here and talk with you." I got up and gave him a hug.

After a couple of days, it was time for me to head back home. My dad took me to the airport and said, "Remember what I said, son. Don't dwell on what you can't change in the past; comprehend it and consider what you can do differently in the future."

"Thank you, Dad. I will make sure to remember it," I responded.

I got on my flight and headed back to Vegas.

As I arrived at the casino, I called Carlo to tell him I was back. He said, "Come by my office tomorrow around 3 pm."

I replied, "Okay." Then went back to my house and relaxed for the night.

Chapter 7

T he next day, I drove to the casino to meet with Carlo. I went into his office, where he was sitting. As always, Evelyn was standing next to him, being flirty with me as I was trying to avoid eye contact with her.

Carlo said to me, "Have a seat, Will. An event is happening today at the casino, and I would like you to accompany miss Evelyn and me."

"What event is going on today?" I asked.

"That is a surprise. Evelyn will escort you to the room I got for you. A tailor is waiting to get measurements, and he's going to get a suit made up; I want you to have the finer things when we enjoy our night."

I looked over to Evelyn as she winked and blew me a kiss. As beautiful as she is, the thought that she was one of the reasons why my relationship has broken up makes her unattractive to me. Maybe she sees that in me and still tries to pounce on me, or she is that friendly to everyone. As Evelyn and I headed to the room, we talked briefly. I asked her, "Can you give me a little info on the event that's going on later?"

Evelyn laughed, "You know I can't do that. It is the boss's surprise for you to find out."

We had a small silent moment, and then she said, "You know, after the event, I am free. This room was booked for you for the rest of the night."

As she said this, I could see her biting her lip as if it was supposed to persuade me to invite her over.

I stopped walking and grabbed her hand, "Look, you are a gorgeous woman. But I don't think this would work out between you and me. My eyes are set on one person and one person only. She will return to me, and I will have my life back."

I let her hand drop and started walking again. Evelyn caught up to me and replied, "You are playing hard to get. I will break you, and you won't be thinking of her ever again. Besides, I'm here right now, and she isn't. That should tell you something, right?"

I kept walking as if I was ignoring her, but she kept bugging me until I answered, "We work together! Shouldn't that mean something to you. I don't want to screw my co-worker, especially with someone I don't know what foreign place in-between those legs have been."

Evelyn grabbed my hand to stop me from walking. As I turned around to look at her, I saw a palm coming from the left side of my face. SMACK! That knocked me back some and almost made me fall down. She can pack a mean swing in that arm.

I held the side of my face and asked, "What was that for?!"

"Better keep up, so you know what room yours is!"

We got to the room, and Evelyn said while crossing her arms, "I'll be waiting for you out here. Once you are done, I am tasked to escort you back to Carlo's office."

I smiled and said, "Okay."

As I entered the room, you could see Evelyn roll her eyes when I said that.

After the tailor got my measurements, we headed back to the office.

Evelyn was walking faster than before; I think I pissed her off. I kind of felt bad; maybe I should apologize. If I do that, she'll think I am interested, which I'm not. I'll just let it be and move on.

Since Evelyn was in front of me, I tried to look away at the surrounding things and not pay attention to her. But my eyes kept crawling back and checking her out. I wanted to slap myself, so I didn't get distracted, but I gave in. "Hey, I'm sorry. I apologize for saying that rude thing to you back there. It was unnecessary."

Evelyn came to an abrupt stop, and I almost walked into her. I exclaimed, "Woah, what's wrong?! You stopped so fast, I almost ran into you."

I could feel the rage coming from Evelyn even though she wasn't looking at me. I tapped her shoulder and said, "Evelyn, you there?"

Out of nowhere, she turns around and puts her arms around me. She throws me against the wall and starts to kiss me seductively. Kissing my lips to my neck, back to my lips. She smiled and whispered, "I knew you would come around."

I kept myself from kissing her back, grabbed her arms, and said, "Hey, this isn't the place for it." I thought to myself, that isn't the right thing to say. Damnit, Will, think before you speak next time.

Evelyn stops kissing me and says, "So, are you inviting me to your room afterward?"

I just got myself into a huge mess. I need a way out now; I can't just leave it like this. Remember, Will, think before you speak.

I replied, "Let's see how things go tonight."

No Will, damnit, Will. What are you doing? You are supposed to run the other way, not into the fire headfirst. You need to stop what you're doing and rethink your motive.

Evelyn looks at me flirtatiously and says, "Okay big boy!" She grabs my penis through my pants and adds, "I'll be waiting for the both of you."

She then walks away and continues, "Come on, Carlo is waiting."

I feel like I was just rushed by a rhino and pinned to the wall. I don't want to keep going; I want to run away forever to escape this predicament. I hear Evelyn, further down the hallway, "Are you coming, or should I make you come so you're ready for tonight?"

What did I just get myself into? I keep falling into these situations that I shouldn't be in.

We arrived back at Carlo's office. He was on the phone with someone, and his conversation wasn't too pretty. His tone and waving of his hands as he was saying each word looked like he was chewing someone out.

Once he noticed that we had returned, he hung up the phone, and his aggravated face turned into a happy, smiling face. It was like watching a kid walk into a candy store.

"Oh good, my two favorite people are back," Carlo said. "Since we are waiting for the tailor to finish your suit, let us grab a bite to eat."

I thought that was a great idea because I hadn't eaten anything all day yet and was starving.

Then I remembered what happened in the hallway with Evelyn and couldn't help but ask, "Just the three of us?"

Evelyn gave me this death stare that could turn your soul to stone.

Carlo stopped walking, turned to me, and said, "Unless you got a hot date you want to invite, it'd be the three of us. Now come on, I'm starving, and I need a drink. How about you?"

I replied, "Yeah, I'm starving too."

Carlo laughed, wrapped his arm around my shoulder, and proceeded to walk with me. I can feel the death stare still attached to me, but I'm too afraid to glance over and look at Evelyn.

We went to a restaurant inside the casino called Heaven's Garden. It looked very fancy and elegant inside. The host saw Carlo and did not hesitate to say, "Your table is all set for you."

That was the fastest I had ever seen someone get a table in my life. I guess perks of having your own business. I thought to myself, one day, that'll be me when I have my own business.

We got to our table and sat down; my eyes became big when I saw the plates everyone had. These plates indubitably looked like they cost over $100.

A waiter came over with a towel over his arm and politely introduced himself to us. Then he proceeded to grab our wine glasses one by one. He wiped the inside, pointed it towards the light, and placed it back down softly.

He gave us a menu and said, "Please, take your time and let me know if there is anything I can get you."

Before the waiter took a step, Carlo blurted out, "Bring out some of my Pinot Grigio from my cellar, please."

"Of course, sir, right away," the waiter responded. "Anything else I can bring for the table?"

I was stunned by the glance I took at the menu and couldn't get a word out to the waiter. After a couple of seconds, all I could get out and say was, "I'll take some water."

I could hear Carlo laughing, and I noticed Evelyn with her palm on her forehead as she shook her head.

I seriously didn't fit in at this restaurant, and I had never been to a place so exquisite as this one.

Then the thought popped in my head as I sat there; Karina would have loved being in a restaurant like this one.

Here I go, sitting with two other people having these thoughts. Maybe a drink is what I needed.

Before the waiter left, I said to him, "You know what? I'll take the water, but I'll also have what Carlo is drinking."

The waiter nodded and said, "Indeed, right away."

Still smirking, Carlo said, "I am going to go out on a whim and say this is your first time in a 5-star restaurant."

I put my palm to my forehead and replied to Carlo, "Was it that obvious?" Carlo and Evelyn hysterically started laughing as I said that.

In all honestly, for me, this is a luxury being at a place like this. Some people casually come here like it's nothing, but if I tried to eat here without knowing Carlo or being part of his group. I would only get one meal a week with prices like this.

The waiter came back, and we placed our order in. Carlo put his hands together as if he was going to start praying but said, "Will, have you ever had a tailor make you a suit before?"

"No, honestly, I didn't know what that was until I got to the room, and he had his tape measure all around me."

"Things are going to be different from now on. I'm going to care for you like your family, and it is just how I do things around here."

"Well, thank you. It is very appreciated, and I never had service or courtesy given to me like this. It feels good to receive it but also like a dream."

Carlo said, "Give it some time, and you will get used to it."

After some conversations and waiting, our food came out. We began to eat, drink, and have a good time.

As we finished our third bottle of wine, Carlo received a phone call and told us, "Give me a second; I'll be right back."

I thought to myself, oh boy, here we go again. Alone with Evelyn, thank God there are people around this time.

I kept my head down, but something was telling me to pick it up. I looked up, and my eyes automatically went over to Evelyn. She wasn't paying any attention to me, which was good. I turned away, but slowly my head went back to her again.

No Will! You don't need to head in that direction, I thought. It doesn't matter how lonely you are; that is a path you should not follow.

I can't stop watching Evelyn as she is seductively swaying her head, making her hair slowly fly from left to right. I said to myself, look at all the beauty and passion. I start to daydream and become lost in her motions.

Evelyn said to me, giggling, "If your jaw drops any further, it's going to hit the table."

I shook my head to come back to reality. My first instinct was to say, "Huh?"

Evelyn replied, "Wow, you were so lost over here that you forgot your train of thought or what's the saying, your equilibrium is off. You might as well give me your eyes, so I can place them in my purse."

"I am sorry, I was off in a dream world thinking of home."

"You are a horrible liar; you know that, right?"

"Yeah, whatever. I wasn't lying, I think you were trying to seductively get my attention on purpose, and it failed."

Who am I kidding, right? Every ounce of my attention was all over that beautiful woman.

Evelyn bites her lip, winks her eye at me, and then sits in the chair beside me. She puts her hand on the inside of my thigh. My first reaction was to jump, but her tight grip made me sit still.

Evelyn said provocatively, "I already felt big willy. It's on the other Will to let him loose."

I took a big gulp, put my hand on her hand to try to move it, and nervously said, "How about we take this a little slower. Let's get to know each other first."

Evelyn removed her hand from my thigh and turned her body toward me. "Wait a minute, why do I feel like you're a virgin? Did your girl not put out or give it up? No, that can't be right; you have a daughter so you must have experienced it at least once in your life. Do I intimidate you?"

I was upset that she would say things about Karina like that.

I stood up from the table, looked at Evelyn as I was holding in my anger, and said, "You don't know anything about Karina. Don't you ever disrespect her like that. We had a lot of sex; she was the greatest at everything. Just because we had a fallout, you want to come in and keep ruining it for me. I still love her and will love her till I die. And yes, Ashley is my daughter."

I sat back down and took some sips of my wine. My hand was trembling from how furious I was.

I can't believe I just said that out loud and made a scene like that. I looked over at Evelyn; her jaw was about as low as mine when I checked her out.

Evelyn said, "So you have had sex with only one person in your lifetime, and now I see why you are overprotective of her. She is the only person you know and is comfortable with. Let me tell you something, baby; I know a thing or two, and I can show you that I can make you comfortable."

"Oh my god," I said as I put my palm onto my forehead and started shaking my head.

All you hear is laughter coming from Evelyn, but it isn't a burst of humiliating laughter. It felt like a playful laugh that she didn't want to make me mad again.

Evelyn continued, "Look, on a serious note, I understand, okay. I also want you to understand it's okay. We need to hang out more so you can see how easy it is to become comfortable with me."

"How about we table this conversation for another day and enjoy tonight?"

Evelyn smiles and grabs her wine glass, "Okay, cheers for a joyful night."

I grabbed my glass and we touched them together, "Cheers!"

Carlo returns from his phone call and says, "Well, it looks like you guys got the party started without me."

Evelyn and I both laugh at the same time. Then Carlo adds, "I got a call from the tailor and said your suit is ready. Let's wrap this up, and I'll meet you guys in the event center."

Evelyn said to me in an arousing tone, "Let's go put a suit on you."

This feeling I was having felt good; I was having a good time. Maybe, I was drunk from the wine, or this time with Evelyn and Carlo was what I needed.

We arrived at the room, and Evelyn said, "I'll wait for you to get ready. Don't keep me waiting too long."

I wasn't thinking straight and told Evelyn, "Well, I got to make sure this suit fits first and then make sure it looks good on me. So, why don't you come in and be the judge of my outfit."

Evelyn giggled, "Okay."

Wait a minute, what did I just tell her? No, damnit, Will! I can't take it back now. She's already coming into the room; I can't just say stop! I change my mind! I'm not that type of person. But what if she tries something or worse, what if I try something? Oh Will, what did you do?

We entered the room, and the tailor was beside the bed. Evelyn said, "I'll sit here and wait."

The tailor said to the both of us, "Do I need to wait outside for you and the misses?

Quickly, I responded to the tailor, "Misses? Oh no, no, no, no, we aren't together. She is just a friend or co-worker if you'd say."

Evelyn was having the time of her life with this. The only thing you hear from her is laughter.

I looked at Evelyn and said, "I'm glad you're having a good time."

I changed out of my clothes and into the suit. Everything fits, and nothing feels tight anywhere.

I turned to face Evelyn and asked her, "Well, what do you think?"

Evelyn rolled her tongue in a sexy way, then replied, "Hot damn, you looked good in casual clothes but dressed up! Mr. tailor, sir, I think we'll need the room to ourselves now."

"What?! Wait! No! Please! No! Don't leave me alone with her," I said to the tailor.

The tailor laughed and said, "My job is done here. Tell Carlo the check will be in the mail."

He had left, and then we were alone again. Awkward moments when we are alone together like this. I am getting nervous in this room that my back is starting to sweat profusely.

Evelyn comes up to me, puts her hand on my cheek, and says, "We have two hours until we need to meet up with Carlo. I don't know about you, but I need to take a shower. I brought some clothes with me, and I'm going to use your shower, okay."

My eyes became big. Do I let Evelyn into my shower? What's going to happen if she showers here?

The sweat was starting to dry up, and my back felt sticky. Yeah, I need to shower too, but I'm not going in after or before Evelyn.

Evelyn's eyes were seductively looking at me as she slowly started to undress. She stripped down to her lingerie. My eyes became more prominent than before as I couldn't peel them from her body. I felt some drool coming down from the side of my mouth.

"Easy there, Fido," Evelyn said as she wiped the drool away. "Are you going to join me? We don't have much time for the both of us to take a shower after the other."

Do I go to this event sticky from all this sweat? Do I go in the shower with this goddess of a lady? Do I drop the shield that I was carrying?

She took her bra off, and two voluptuous breasts came free and stared right at me. She then took her panties off and turned away from me.

She then looked over her shoulder and placed her finger on her bottom lip. "Oops, I accidentally took everything off," Evelyn said flirtatiously.

I can't do this; I can't look at Karina if I were to do this. Do I just run out of the room? Do I tell her to meet me at the event after her shower? Do I leave knowing that her body is amazingly shaped the way it is? No, this isn't it. This isn't how all of this was supposed to happen.

Evelyn turned to face me and started walking toward me. My body felt numb, and I couldn't move anything. She put her arms around my neck, pulled me closer to her, and kissed me on the lips. I couldn't do anything but stand there and kiss her back.

Evelyn bit my bottom lip as I kissed her back and enticingly said, "Ooooooo, you're finally kissing me!"

She started to undress me by unbuttoning my shirt. Then quickly undid my belt and my pants. I don't know how I moved, but I was able to get my legs free from my pants and toss them on the bed. My shirt was then projected onto the bed, along with the underwear and socks that I was wearing.

"Oh my!" Evelyn said as she looked at my penis.

She grabbed my hand and walked me into the shower with her. Evelyn gradually started to bathe me with soap as I did her.

Our lips were locked together again as she caressed my chest. Evelyn then turned around with her back on me. She grabbed my penis and put it into her vagina. Moans of pleasure roared from Evelyn as she enjoyed each minute with me.

Intense feelings shot up and down my body as I had never felt before. With each push I gave, the moans grew louder and more robust.

I knew when Evelyn had reached her climax from how shaky her legs got as she almost fell down in the shower. I wrapped my arms around her to hold her up, and then she threw her hands onto the wall. She bent over halfway and pushed her butt onto me, making me give her a couple deeper thrusts. I let go of where I had my arms wrapped around, and we went on for what felt like an eternity.

I reached my climax, and I felt like she sucked all the energy right out of my body when she took my penis out of her vagina.

She turned around so that her head was lying on my chest. Evelyn then wrapped her arms around my waist and pulled me closer to her. The water was flowing down from her hair onto my chest.

No-no-no-no-no. Damnit Will, what are you thinking? This is not how it was supposed to happen. What about Karina? Are you going to look at her the same way? I released a frustrated scream inside of my head.

I looked at Evelyn and quickly said, "I need to leave; I have to get out of here!"

Evelyn looked at me with a satisfied smirk and said, "That's fine; I got what I wanted."

Evelyn pushed off from my chest and exited the shower. She then grabbed all her clothes, got dressed, and left the room.

I stood in the shower, naked, as the water hit my chest. I couldn't move, think, or even say anything.

What have I done? I ended up doing the very thing I told myself not to do.

I finally came to my senses, turned off the water, exited the shower, and stood beside my bed. Everything happened so fast, and I was still trying to process it.

I glanced over at the clock. Shit, I only have thirty minutes to get ready and be downstairs. I grabbed all my clothes, got dressed, and left my room.

I made my way to the elevator, glancing at my reflection from the chrome doors. I wanted to punch those doors, but I kept my composure.

Why isn't this elevator moving?! I looked at the button; damnit Will, you never pressed the button. My mind isn't currently there; I must get it together before meeting with Carlo. He can't see me like this; what will he think?

I arrived at the lobby, and many people were waiting to enter the event center. I walked to the entrance, where a bouncer directed people around with a clipboard. He got to me, placed his clipboard down, and said, "The boss's right-hand man, we've been expecting your arrival. Please, this way, follow me."

I followed him to a seating room with Carlo sitting there alone. I thought to myself, good, Evelyn hasn't made it yet. I walked over to Carlo, placed my hand on his shoulder, and said, "Hey Carlo, made it. This is a very nice suit, by the way. The tailor wanted me to tell you the check would be in the mail."

Carlo looked over at me and snickered. He turned his head back to where he was initially looking.

Something doesn't seem right with Carlo. He isn't his energetic self that you see every day.

I'm trying not to think about what happened back in the room, so I try to make a conversation with Carlo.

"So, what is this event that was a surprise?" I asked Carlo.

He grabbed his glass from the table, took a sip, and placed it back down. He stared into the distance at some lights shining over something in the event center. I couldn't tell if he was observing the scenery or just trying to look for someone.

I was going to ask Carlo another question when I felt a hand softly touch my back. Then a voice called out to me, "I'm glad you decided to come out and join us. I get to see this handsome face again."

I turned around, and it was Evelyn behind me. I was hoping not to see her again after all that happened. She winked her eye at me, blew me a kiss, and sat down next to Carlo.

Carlo noticed Evelyn sitting next to him, turned around to me, and said, "Oh great, the both of you are here now. From the sounds of things, you guys had a "formal" meeting together."

Oh jeez, he learned of the little thing we had earlier. I stood there like a deer in front of a moving vehicle. I didn't think he knew about it. Am I in trouble for it? No, of course not; why would I be? Evelyn initiated it; she was the reason why it happened. She forced it onto me, and I couldn't do anything about it.

Carlo added, "How about getting this meeting started before the event commences?"

I sat beside Carlo on the chair next to him, opposite Evelyn. I looked over to Carlo and said, "So, what is this surprise event you have for me?"

Carlo waved his arm out in front and said, "This is the surprise I have for you. Today is an epic day that we host a pay-per-view boxing fight. Two of the biggest names in their weight class are going head-to-head in the main event. Do you know how much money this brings into the casino? Not just from the boxers and all the other things in between. But from the fans that place wagers on all these events."

I looked amazed at everything around me; I had never been to anything like this. So many people, security guards, and vendors bartering food or clothing items. I had no idea something like this even existed. I could get used to something like this, I thought.

As I admired the scenery, Carlo nudged me and said, "I'll tell you how all of this works later, but there's a matter at hand, Will. I recently did some numbers from the casino and found a slight problem. I notice that you have a large amount due to the casino from betting.

"Now I know you're my right-hand man, so I'm not gunning for your head just yet. If you're going to be involved with what I have going on, I need you to not have an outstanding balance like this one. Just because you're doing jobs for me doesn't mean that money will help. There's only so much I can do for you until it's time to collect."

Evelyn butted into our conversation and said enticingly, "Send him over to me; I'll put him to work."

Carlo looked over at Evelyn with a confused look and said, "So he bangs you for what, free? Or are you going to pay off his balance each time he screws you?"

Evelyn sat back with her arms crossed and stuck her lip out as if she was pouting. She really is into me bad. For what? I'm not that special for someone to be obsessed with me like that.

Carlo looked back at me and said, "With that being said, I have something that may help you loosen some of that debt if your game. It won't clear the whole total, but it will help some."

I replied to Carlo, "Okay, I am game. What is it?

Carlo responded, "I have a slight problem with a competitor down the street. He also has a casino as big as this one and thinks he is better. From what I heard recently, he has been sending people to snoop around my casino, and I don't know why.

"I need you to do some snooping of your own and see what you can find out. Maybe, head over to his casino and do some searching. They know Evelyn is part of my crew, so I can't send her. Since you are new, they don't know that you work for me yet. I say we use this to our advantage."

"What if they do know me? And what if I get caught? I'm sure he wouldn't like the fact that someone is snooping around his casino. You don't want to lose someone eminent to him, right?"

Carlo started to rub his chin and thought for a couple minutes. "Yeah, you're right. Let's find another way, but what though?"

I turned my head to look at Evelyn and automatically thought club manager. There has to be some sort of club he owns, and I can try to get some information out of there.

I told Carlo, "He must have some other kind of entertainment venue he owns, right?"

Carlo nodded, smiled, and said, "Now you're on to something. I like it, let me do my research, and I'll get back to you on that."

Carlo then gets out of his chair and turns his attention towards the middle of the center again. He grabs his glass that the waiter just brought and turns to Evelyn and me. He lifted his glass and said, "Let's enjoy this spectacular night and have a good time!"

We all took a drink and I said to myself, that tasted good. I looked at the bottle sitting in the ice bucket.

I asked Evelyn, "This looks like a very fancy bottle."

She laughs and says to me, "That's because it is a very, very expensive bottle of bubbly."

Bubbly? What does that even mean? I had never heard of that term used before. Is it made from bubbles or something? There is a lot to learn about the life I never had outside of Karina.

I asked Evelyn, "What is bubbly?"

She placed her hand on her forehead and shook her head.

Carlo sat between Evelyn and me, extended his arms, pulled us together, and said, "Will, you have become an exclamation mark in my organization. Keep doing what you're doing, and you'll go far. There is one thing I need to talk to you about since Evelyn is here."

I replied, "Of course; what is it, boss?"

Carlo said, "When Evelyn first took the job of club manager. I was initially skeptical, but then time passed, and I started to see this seed grow into a beautiful rose. She surged from ashes to become an influential leader.

"After I had seen that, I had her pledge an oath to me. An oath of honor must be made if you are ever in a bind, a pinch, or a decisive decision. If this situation means joining someone else's group other than mine, you will choose death over dishonor. So, death before dishonor is the pledge."

I looked at Carlo with a concerned and confused look. I turned my attention to Evelyn, who had an enormous smile.

I turned back to Carlo, and before I could say anything, he told me, "Before you take this pledge, I want you to know something. To live is the greatest thing in the world. But to die for honor is one of the heaviest burdens one can hold on their shoulders. So, I want you to take a heavy consideration of what you pledge before doing it."

I said to Carlo, "Why did you need Evelyn here for you to say that?"

Carlo responded, "For a witness to see the oath being pledged. Exactly how we did it when Evelyn took the oath. It is a long story, but that is a conversation for another time. A lady named April was with me when Evelyn had taken her pledge."

I took a deep breath, exhaled, and said to Carlo, "I pledge my loyalty to you. I will take the oath of honor and will not bring shame to you."

Carlo smiled, laughed, and said, "Good, now let's drink and have an amazing time. I see plenty more of these moments coming for us."

After the event, Carlo said to Evelyn and me, "I am going to clock out for the night and head out. I will see you guys later."

He then turned to me and said, "Don't have too much fun with her." As he winks at me and points in Evelyn's direction.

He patted me on the shoulder and exited the event center.

I didn't want to make the moment awkward, so I left the center without saying bye to Evelyn.

I got about halfway down the lobby when I felt someone grab my arm. I looked back to see who it was, and Evelyn had gripped my arm. How do I get away from this situation now?

Evelyn looked at me with these sad puppy eyes and said, "Look, all I want to do is apologize for earlier. I took advantage of you and knew I shouldn't have done that. You are highly fragile right now, and I used that towards my selfishness. Well, I mean, it was a good time, and I can't complain.

"But we need to be partners in this organization. To be successful, we must learn how to work together. We also need to be a team and cooperative with each other. I don't mind messing around occasionally but with a degree of respect for you and me. Sounds fair?"

I looked at her, and I couldn't say anything. Why is this a familiar feeling every time she is around me? How is she able to make me feel like this? What did I do to deserve this? She is a gorgeous lady and is deeply obsessed with me for some odd reason.

Evelyn's puppy eyes faded, and her face started to turn angry. She punched my chest and said, "Well, are you going to say anything to me or even recognize that I told you any of that?" She placed her hands on her hips, started tapping the floor with her foot, and patiently awaited my answer.

What do I tell her? I don't want to make any mistakes if Karina comes back into my life. I don't want to casually throw us away like it was a beaten-up rag doll. I must think about the future and what holds for me with Karina.

I grabbed one of her hands, held it, and said, "So much has happened within a short period. I had seen my girlfriend leave with my daughter for my poor choices. I saw my boss shot in the head from a decision that I could not make up. People have been dying left and right in front of me, and I don't know what I'm doing here yet. I am sorry, I can't answer your question truthfully yet. But, yes, we need to cooperate as a team for us to succeed."

I let go of her hand and looked down at the floor in shame. Then she places her hand under my chin to lift my head. She smiled and said, "Go get some sleep, and maybe we will see each other tomorrow."

She gave me a kiss on the cheek, walked out of the casino, and then vanished from my sight. I walked over to the elevator and headed upstairs.

I entered my room, took my suit off, and got into bed. My body was exhausted after this day, and sleep sounded terrific. I turned off the lamp on my nightstand and went to sleep.

Chapter 8

With that day behind me, I went downstairs to meet with Carlo. He wanted me to come to talk to him in his office after the call I received from him this morning. I wonder what this is all about, I thought.

As I got to Carlo's office, I saw Carlo sitting behind his desk and Evelyn sitting on the opposite side. I went over to them and sat down next to Evelyn.

"What's up, boss?" I asked.

Carlo said, "I have to send Evelyn away for a few days, and I want you to accompany her."

I thought, oh great. A few days? What am I supposed to do with Evelyn as we stay together? Is this the part where he bluntly starts laughing and tells us, "I am only kidding! You are not residing in the same house." Come on, Carlo, please don't do this to me.

Then, Carlo gets out of his chair, looks at me, and says, "You look like you want to add something to this. Care to enlighten us with your thoughts."

This man had just put me in the spotlight, and he could read my face and my thoughts. I could hear Evelyn next to me chuckling.

Carlo says, "Is there a problem with the task I gave you? Do you think turning down my mission would be a bright idea? I think you need to get your priorities straight and remember, you work for me now. Just because you became startled by a couple of gunshots doesn't mean I will take it easy on you. That is not how I conduct my business." Carlo then looked at me with a smile and continued to say, "So, is there a problem?"

I replied, "No, there isn't one. I'm sorry, sir." I feel like I was just scolded by my father as if I did something wrong. This man knew how to put the fear of God in you while smiling. I continued, "Where in Vegas are we going?"

"You're not staying in Vegas; you guys are flying to Houston, Texas. There is a package that Evelyn needs to pick up, which can't be delivered by mail. That is why I am sending her there, and I want you to be her bodyguard. Make sure nothing happens to her while she is obtaining this package."

I turned to Evelyn and said, "Well, you ready, honey?"

Carlo falls back into his chair, puts his palm to his forehead, and shakes his head. I saw Evelyn get out of her chair and walk to the door. She then says, "I'll be waiting in the lobby for you. Get your stuff ready and see me once you are finished." She opens the door, exits the room, and slams the door on the way out."

I looked over to Carlo and said, "Was it something I said?"

Carlo laughed and replied, "Women! You can't live with them, and you can't live without them. You better get a move on it and don't keep the lady waiting too long. It wouldn't be a nice weekend getaway if you made her mad by waiting."

I got up from my chair and headed for the exit. Carlo stops me at the door and yells out, "All jokes aside, both of you, please be safe out there. I know she can handle herself, but make sure nothing happens to her."

I nodded my head to agree and exited the room. I closed the door, stood there for a moment, and started to think about what could go wrong.

So many negative things popped into my head as I stood there. Maybe, I'm overthinking the whole situation. I am sure we will be fine with both of us. Let's hurry and get my stuff together to keep her from waiting.

I drove home and started packing up my clothes and things. I opened my closet, and one of Ashley's toys fell from the top shelf. The toy hit the ground and made a funny sound. I looked at the toy, and emotions started to flow through my body.

Images of the three of us playing at the park, enjoying some ice cream, and many others ran through my mind. I sat on the bed and let a couple of tears fall as I thought about everything. So many good memories, but I dread the decision I had made here.

All for what, extra money? Whatever it is that we have to do these next couple of days. You have to be wise with your choices. Don't let them cause another downward spiral to happen in your life.

I got up from the bed, put the toy back on the shelf, and closed the door. I told myself, Karina will return, Will. Just stay positive through it all and be patient. I grabbed my bags and left the house.

I headed for a place that Karina and I would take Ashley to. I pulled into the parking lot, sat in my vehicle, and gazed at the building. This establishment had trampolines inside, and we would jump almost all day.

There I was again, dropping a tear from reminiscing. I looked at the clock and noticed I had wasted nearly two hours.

Evelyn is going to kill me before we can get to do the mission. I told myself I got to get back to the casino.

I arrived back at the casino and entered the lobby. Evelyn greeted me as she yelled, "You took your sweet ass time, didn't you? I thought maybe you ran off, and I would have to do this on my own."

Evelyn signaled to a bell boy with a luggage cart, and he took it outside and started loading a vehicle with them.

I looked at her bags and said, "What are you doing staying a whole week at a spa resort?"

Evelyn rolls her eyes as she walks past me and says, "Have valet park your car with Carlo's. We are getting chauffeured to the airport." She got to the passenger door, turned around to look at me, and yelled, "Well, aren't you going to open it for me?"

I hung my head in shame and thought, it's going to be a long couple of days.

We got into the vehicle and took off. For some reason, I felt comfortable as Evelyn sat next to me. I wanted to look over at her, but I did not want it to look obvious what I was doing.

As time passed, I found myself gazing at Evelyn's dress. "You like what you see; I have the same dress in gray too," Evelyn said.

I quickly looked up and said, "Huh? What are you talking about? I was uh…. looking at the floor."

Evelyn replied humorously, "Yeah, sure, whatever you say."

We got to the airport, but Evelyn had the driver take us around the side instead of dropping us off at the entrance.

I asked. "Where are we going?"

"We're getting on our plane."

We pulled up next to a jet with 'Flying Queen' on the side. I asked, "A private jet? Yeah right, I thought we were flying economy."

Evelyn answered, "Well, yeah, you think someone like me is flying with a hundred other people. Nope, this classy lady gets a jet all to herself."

She walked towards me, grabbed my cheek, and continued, "And my handsome bodyguard gets to join me."

We loaded the jet and took off. The inside of this jet was so luxurious and exquisite. Huge flat-screen TVs on the wall with a bar in the middle of the cabin. I have never been in something like this before.

Evelyn calls out to me, "Come here, Will. I want to discuss some things over with you."

I went and sat at the table where she was. Evelyn brought out a map with highlighted places as I sat there. Then she said, "Okay, the place we are staying is here. We will stay there tonight, then meet with the guy at this place tomorrow."

She continued to talk, and my mind faded away, gazing at Evelyn as she spoke. She talked so smoothly and used each body motion to describe the steps. I think gradually; I was catching feelings for her. No, Will, get your head back together. We are here for one purpose, and that's for nothing to go wrong.

"Okay, did you understand everything?" Evelyn asked.

"Huh?" I zoned out and didn't hear the rest of what she had to say. Oh great, Will you surely need to get it together.

Evelyn enticingly approached me and placed her hand on my chest. "You know, we could ditch our quick briefing and enjoy another night to ourselves."

Embarrassed, I stuttered, "I think we should go over what you had said."

"Then get it together!" Evelyn pushed off my chest and continued flirtatiously, "Or I will have to do some naughty things to you." We got back to discussing what was going to happen.

Our flight landed, and a limousine was waiting for us. We unloaded the jet and made our way to the house we would be staying at.

We arrived at the house, and a man leaning on a car was waiting for us. We got out, and the man said, "The ever-so gorgeous Evelyn, how are you? It has been a while; it's good to see you."

Evelyn replied, "It is good to see you too, Simon. Yes, it has been a while. This man next to me is Will, who will be accompanying me on my mission."

"Ah yes, the recruit that Carlo promoted to chief assistant during his interview. Your name is widely known out here once news broke free. It's a pleasure to make your acquaintance. Quite the power out here having both right hands in one household." Simon responded.

I replied, "It's good to meet you too."

Simon threw me a set of keys and said, "These are the keys to the vehicle in the garage. You break it; you're responsible for replacing it. Everything should be set for you both as requested."

After getting settled in, we decided to get something to eat. We drove to a restaurant that Evelyn knows.

We entered the restaurant, and a man said gleefully, "The marvelous Evelyn, glad to bask in your presence again. How many today?"

"Good to see you, Sean. Only two today," Evelyn replied.

Sean looked at me and asked Evelyn flirtatiously, "Oowee, who is this yummy masculine fellow you have here?"

I turned to Evelyn with a confused look. Is this guy hitting on me? And what does he mean by yummy? Is he going to eat me like a cannibal or something? A little help here, Evelyn.

Evelyn responded, "He's off-limits, so don't even think about it. He's my co-worker and partner in a mission the boss sent us on."

Sean said, "Oooooo girl, you done already claimed this one, didn't you? You can't hide that face from me; I know you too well."

I couldn't believe they were talking about me when I was right next to them. So I butted into Evelyn and Sean's conversation and said, "How about we go sit down somewhere!"

Sean laughed and said, "Mmhmmm, and he's feisty. Girl, you betta put a ring on him." Then, he walked us to our table and said, "Enjoy, my loves."

I looked at Evelyn and said, "What was all that about? And what does he mean by yummy? Was he going to eat me? Like an animal or something?"

Evelyn let out a big laugh and replied, "Oh, Sean would have done more than eat you. Trust me, I saved you from him. You should be thanking me. Just go along with it and act like your mine. You'll be safe from harm if you do that."

Sean came back to the table with a pen and pad. I quickly asked Evelyn, "Are you ready to order, honey?"

As I said that, Evelyn dropped her head and shook it in shame.

Sean replied, "I'll come back in a bit."

"Honey?!" Evelyn exclaimed. "You have to sell it for it to work."

I responded, "I know what I'm doing; remember, I was a salesman."

Sean returned and asked, "So what can I get the lovely dual started for drinks?"

Evelyn quickly responded, "Let's do some wine; I feel like a good Sauvignon Blanc would lighten the mood."

The way she said the name of that wine was so exquisite. I found myself lost in thought, gazing at Evelyn as she lusciously sat there. I couldn't pull my eyes away. The events from the hotel room flashed in my head.

Then I heard Evelyn yell, "Will!"

I returned to reality and saw Evelyn and Sean looking at me. Oh lord, I was absent-minded, and I don't know what all happened. Were they trying to get my attention, and I wasn't answering?

I looked at Evelyn, confused, and she said, "Sean asked you a question three times, and you never answered. What do you want to drink?"

I looked at Sean and said, "I'll have what she's having."

Sean put his hand to his mouth and replied, "Oh... my... gosh.... Girl, no you didn't! You have done already gave him some--."

Evelyn's face became red. "Hush, go get the wine."

Sean placed his hand on Evelyn's shoulder and giggled, "You're going to have to tell me every juicy detail later, Evi." Then walked away from the table.

I was confused about what was going on. Evelyn stopped Sean before he could finish, and I wanted to hear what he had to say.

I asked Evelyn, "Why didn't you let him finish? And why did your face turn red?"

"Don't worry about it! Focus on what you're going to order!"

She grabs the menu and hides her face. I was still confused about everything, and I stared at Evelyn. I could see her moving the menu aside to see if I was still looking and then bringing it back to hide her face.

After we ate our dinner, we took off back to the house. I went into my room and saw Evelyn go into hers. I lay on the bed, looking at the ceiling, and thought about everything.

As I was thinking, I felt something touching my leg. I looked and saw Evelyn slowly walking into the room. Oh great, is she going to do the same thing again? Evelyn jumped in bed next to me, became comfy and said, wrap your arm around me, please."

Evelyn sighed, then said, "My dad was a drunk, and he beat my mom numerous times. I remember waking up in the middle of the night, and the police were there because he beat her badly. My mom and I ran away and moved to another state, and we stayed in Michigan for some time.

"She did what she had to do to support me. Sometimes I woke up in the middle of the night and she wasn't there. I stayed up until she got home and would see her with random guys outside giving her money. I never knew what that was all about.

"But, one day, after she tucked me in, I heard her leave again. I waited for her to come back, but she never returned. Two days passed, and a policeman came to the door to pick me up. He dropped me off at an orphanage, where I resided until I was eighteen.

"I hitchhiked on a semi to Vegas, where I saw Carlo for the first time. He took me in as his club manager at Oceans Paradise since his other manager was promoted to his right-hand woman. There is more to my story, but that is just the main stuff. Maybe we could sit down another time, and I can tell you everything."

I didn't know what to say; she just suddenly told me her life story, and I never asked. I'm very appreciative that she felt comfortable telling me. It sounded like she had been through a lot in her life. I know I saw a lot in the past few weeks, but nothing like what she has seen in her life.

I said, "Did you ever find out what happened to your mom?"

"She was killed by a man that picked her up that night of her disappearance. I was never told who did it or if they caught the guy."

"Can I ask you a question?"

"You don't have to ask me to ask a question. Just say what is on your mind."

"Why did you tell me all of that."

"I don't know." She placed her head on my chest, snuggled me, and continued, "I feel comfortable now and want to enjoy this feeling with you."

The comfort I felt with her next to me was incredible. I could lay with her for eternity and be content with it. Nothing else mattered around me.

I said, "So, you mentioned another lady that was in your position. Did you know who she was?"

Evelyn replied, "Yeah, she was my mentor and I was next to her when she died."

The moment became silent and then Evelyn asked, "Can I cuddle with you while we sleep?"

"I uh… I don't mind."

"Good, because I wasn't going to move if you told me no."

The way Evelyn caressed my chest as she lay beside me felt soothing and relaxing. I could get used to something like this.

She then pushed off my chest to give me a kiss. It felt as if I was in heaven while we were kissing, and I forgot we were in Texas for the moment.

After the kiss, she gazed into my eyes and said, "Good night, sweet dreams."

Then, placed her head back onto my chest and held me as we fell asleep.

The next day, we arrived at the place where Evelyn needed to meet this guy. It was in a container port with these massive cargo containers stacked on each other.

I've always seen these in the movies but never up close like this. It felt intimidating and overwhelming being next to them. I could only think of them falling over on us as we waited.

From a distance, a car was heading towards us. Evelyn quickly opened the glove compartment and handed me a small handgun.

She said, "Hide this and keep it with you if something happens. I also have one of my own, but you will have a backup if I can't access it."

The vehicle arrived in front of ours, and Evelyn winked at me and said, "Let's go have some fun."

The people in the other car exited their vehicle, so we got out of ours too. An older Hispanic gentleman with a scruffy beard gleamed at us from behind his two bodyguards. He then said something that sounded Spanish to the guards, making them move aside.

The man approached us and said with a heavy accent, "Carlo sends me his heavy hitters to pick up a package. Then expects me to take it easy on you guys." He laughs and continues, "How bout I send both your bodies back to him to send a message? Carlo was too scared to come see me face-to-face."

The man turned around, walked back to his vehicle then stopped once he passed his guards. Evelyn nudged me and whispered, "Get ready."

The man again said something in Spanish to his guards, and you could see them reaching for their weapons.

So we quickly grabbed ours and shot the guards before they could make their move.

The man raised his arms and said, "Okay, very well. The package is yours; tell Carlo to keep the change. I'll see him when I see him." He handed us a package, entered the vehicle, and had his driver take off.

I looked over to Evelyn, and she had a massive smile. My hands were still shaking from adrenaline. Did our plan work to perfection? A man of his stature just handed this over without more of a fight.

I said to Evelyn, "Can we get out of here!?"

She laughed and said, "Yeah, let's go. Our job is done."

We headed back to the house, and my hands were still shaking. Evelyn looked at me with a smile and said, "Don't worry, you'll get used to it, and the shaking will eventually go away."

The night came, and I wanted to lay in bed to relax before we left tomorrow morning.

As I lay there, I saw Evelyn at my door, and she had on a satin two-piece pajama set with shorts that looked amazing on her. She came in, biting her lip, and lay in bed with me again. Evelyn placed her head on my chest and settled her leg across me.

She hugged me tight and said, "One more time before we return to reality. I want to enjoy this as much as possible."

I gave in, wrapped my arm around her, and caressed her. I sighed in relief from how good it felt having her right there with me. Evelyn chuckled but didn't say anything. She grasped me tighter and sighed in comfort too.

Then, she came closer to my face and kissed me gently. Placed her hand on the side of my head, and the gentle kiss turned intimate. Evelyn got up and relaxed her head back onto my chest.

These past days all Evelyn wanted to do was kiss me. I was sure she would attempt something else, but I was wrong.

Being curious, I asked, "Evelyn, how come um.... how come you didn't try seducing me again like the hotel?"

She laughed and started caressing my chest. "You satisfied my needs at the hotel. You made me want you in a different aspect, a deeper one. I'm glad everything went well out here. Our mission was a success, and we spent more time together."

I paused for a second and thought about Karina. Then I responded, "You know I can't be involved in anything profound yet, Karina is still on my mind, and that's not fair to you. I don't want you to get hurt over this."

Evelyn replied, "I'm glad you're thinking of me; that's a step in the right direction. But don't worry, I'm a big girl and everything will work out for us. I know it will; I can feel it. Get some sleep, tomorrow, we leave in the morning, and we'll be back at the casino."

Chapter 9

*I*n the early hours at the house in Texas, Carlo called Evelyn as I was sleeping still. Carlo said to Evelyn, "So far, what do you think about Will? I know you guys had your little rendezvous and whatever you are doing over there. I don't want to know, but I want to know whether he is a good fit in our group?"

Evelyn responded, "He's very fragile right now with the loss of his girl, Fenn, and some other things in his life. His mindset is there, but he doesn't know how to utilize it in this line of work. He did pretty well earlier, I will say that. Did you ever do any research about venues?"

"Good, glad to hear he's starting to come around. I still need to do some research on that. Antonio isn't one to flaunt what he owns; if he does own anything, it might be registered in another name. We obviously need to figure this out before something bad happens."

"I agree. Maybe we shouldn't send him over there. Once we see what venue is in his possession, I can send one of the girls to scope out things. We can afford to lose one of them but not Will, and I'm not saying that for my own satisfaction."

Carlo looked hard at his cup of coffee as he thought about what to do next. There aren't many times when a man of his stature was stomped in a position like this. Of course, with his power, he could send someone to take care of whatever needed to be taken care of. But another casino owner is different, especially one with the same financial success as his own.

Evelyn then said, "What about the underground casino? I'm sure many people talk over there about many things. Couldn't you squeeze some info out of some of them? Better yet, have Will squeeze them to release something vital."

Carlo said, "I mean, it's not a bad idea. But grabbing the wrong person could also mean starting another war that I wouldn't be able to afford to start. Those people over there don't have loyalty to just one place, and that's why it's an underground establishment. Off the records, not found for the naked eye to see."

"Well, we need to start somewhere then. I believe that's our best chance of gaining the edge over this. I'll accompany Will as his partner since he accompanied me on my task."

"If you think this is a good option, why don't we try it out."

"I'll make the preparations once I get back and see that this will get done. After Will wakes up, I'll inform him of what's happening."

"Wait before you hang up, don't tell Will anything. I will talk to Will once you both are back in Vegas."

After that, Carlo hung the phone up.

A couple of hours after Carlo and Evelyn's conversation:

I felt someone shaking me to wake me up and saying, "Hey, we have to get going."

I opened my eyes and thought I saw Karina. I wiped my eyes to get a better view and saw it was Evelyn waking me up. She continued, "Good morning, sleeping beauty. It's time to wake up; the limo will be here in an hour."

I replied, "Damn, how long did I sleep?"

"I don't know, but I slept amazingly next to you," Evelyn responded, then left the room.

I jumped in the shower and got ready for the day to start.

I went over to the window to open the curtains all the way. The sun shone bright, with clear skies a beautiful scenery outside. I took a deep breath in and exhaled to take it all in.

I got everything together and waited in the living room with Evelyn. The limo showed up and took us to the airport to get on the jet again.

We flew into Vegas and arrived at the casino.

I told Evelyn, "I'm taking my stuff to my house, and I'll meet you later." She nodded to agree.

Before we both walked away, we heard Carlo say, "Alright, the both of you are back. Once settled in, come to my office, and I have something for you, Will. Oh and the same hotel room you had before is available to you. Why don't you drop your stuff off there and come see me after."

I nodded my head then went to drop my stuff off and made my way to Carlo's office.

I walked into his office and only saw Carlo. I asked, "Where is Evelyn?

"She is on her way," Carlo replied. Then the door opened, and Carlo continued, "Speak of the devil."

Evelyn walked in with a happy smile, and once she heard what Carlo said, it turned into a distasteful look.

She looked at Carlo and me, then said, "Really, you guys? Then you wonder why nobody likes either one of you."

Carlo looked at me and said, "Evelyn and I had a conversation this morning while you were sleeping. We think it's best to send both of you to the underground casino, and I want to see if we could obtain valuable information from someone out there."

I thought to myself, they were on the phone this morning while I was sleeping. I must have been out because I didn't hear anything.

Evelyn glanced at me as I was doing all this thinking. She said, "You're thinking too hard. I can see the smoke coming out of your ears.

I looked at Evelyn and said, "Huh? What are you talking about?"

"Nothing; don't worry about it," Evelyn replied.

I looked at Carlo and said, "When do you need us to go?"

Carlo replied, "Tonight would be great, but I know you just got back from an exhausting trip. If not tonight, then definitely tomorrow."

Evelyn and I looked at each other, and I blurted out, "I don't mind doing it tonight. It gives me something to do other than sit at home."

Still looking at Evelyn, she starts to bite her lip and says, "You just can't get enough of me, can you?"

I shook my head and said, "This is for a good cause. So that we can get intel for Carlo. Besides, you already claimed me from what Sean said."

Evelyn's face turned red, and Carlo let out a boisterous laugh and said, "You took Will to go and see Sean?"

"I was hungry, okay. Besides, I didn't know Sean was still working there," Evelyn responded.

She crossed her arms, stood there, and pouted. Evelyn said, "You guys are mean, ganging up on me like that."

Carlo said, "Well, if you guys are going tonight, I'll call the tailor to get ready to make another suit. I will send him to your room."

I answered, "Can't I just wear some slacks and a nice dress shirt?

"You don't understand, Will," Carlo Said. "Everyone that goes into that casino to play and enjoy themselves has a luxurious presence and manner. I need you to fit in with them to help us get what we need."

I nodded and said, "Okay, I will head upstairs to my room and wait for him."

Carlo said, "Oh, Evelyn, Esmerelda will be waiting for you, and she has a dress she thinks you would love. Let me know once you both are back, and we can go over a plan."

I nodded my head, then Evelyn and I left Carlo's office.

As I was about to walk away, Evelyn grabbed my arm and said, "Why don't we both wait for the tailor? Then, you can come with me so I can get fitted for mine."

I let my head hang after she said that. I don't know if I could go through that again. I am developing feelings but is it the right thing to do. Should I tell her?

I turned to Evelyn and said, "I am—."

Before I could finish, Carlo called my phone, and I answered, "Hey Carlo."

"Your tailor is on his way up," Carlo said. He then hung up the phone.

I looked at Evelyn and said, "The tailor is on his way up to my room." I placed my hands on my head in frustration and shook my head.

Evelyn grabbed my hands and said, "How about this? We place this conversation on hold. I'll accompany you with the tailor, and you can accompany me with the seamstress. We need to have that couple feeling if we are to succeed in the task later."

I nodded my head and said, "Yeah, your right."

I held my arm out for her to grab onto and continued, "Come on, honey."

Evelyn hits my arm and replies, "Stop calling me honey. Change it up or something. Make it something spicy or facetious."

I asked, "Why don't you like being called honey?"

Evelyn answered, "It sounds lame. You need to make it sound intriguing."

We both laughed and headed to my room. Once we arrived, the same tailor was waiting for me by the door.

The tailor says, "It's good to see you and the misses again."

I replied, "She's not the mi—."

Evelyn pinched the back of my arm and had this atrocious look on her face.

"Ow! Really, what was that for?" I asked Evelyn.

The tailor laughed and responded, "Don't worry; as the years go by, you become numb to the pain. Well, that's how it was for the wife and me."

In my head, I said, but she isn't even the misses. Oh wait, the mission, I have to work on acting as if we are a couple.

The tailor says, "Come on, this will only take but a minute. I still have your measurements from last time, but I want to ensure everything is correct."

After the tailor got the measurements and left, we decided to head out and see the seamstress. We arrived at a building called Ezzy's Glamour Boutique. Once inside, I noticed all the dresses and outfits for women. Some of them were so elegant and glimmering, and they must cost a fortune from their appearance.

A lady said to me flirtatiously, "Hello, I am Esmeralda. This is my shop; what can I get for a fine handsome man like yourself?"

Evelyn came over to where I was standing and said, "Hey Ezzy, long time no see. How have you been, girl?"

"Oh hey girl, the business has been amazing since I moved the shop over here," Esmerelda responded.

Evelyn replies, "I see you met my man, Will. Will this is Ezzy, my favorite seamstress in the world and my best friend."

Esmerelda puts her hand over her mouth and says, "Oh my gosh, Evelyn. I did not know that was your man. I am very sorry, Will; I didn't know you came with Evelyn."

Esmerelda gets close to Evelyn and whispers, "Girl, did you already, you know. Give him a small taste of the business? Did you let him lay it down on you?"

"Girl, you already know me. I didn't give him a small taste. I gave him the whole cuisine plus dessert," Evelyn responds.

Esmeralda said, "Oooooo, no you didn't! You done gave him the keys and let him drive."

Evelyn and Esmeralda quickly replied, "And he drove it like he stole it!" Then they laughed simultaneously.

Esmeralda says, "Girl, I miss those days when we get together like this."

"Me too, Ezzy," Evelyn responds. "We need to hook up again; maybe find you a man so we could double date to a ball like old-time sake."

As I was standing there, I could hear them chatting. So I butted into Evelyn and Esmerelda's conversation, "Um, I can hear you both, and a taste of what business?"

Evelyn and Esmerelda laughed rambunctiously.

I looked at Evelyn and asked, "What was that all about?"

"Oh, nothing, just girl talk, don't worry about it," Evelyn answered.

Evelyn stood on a platform and had Esmerelda get measurements and other things for the dress. This looks similar to what the tailor was doing for me. Maybe because of genders, they have to have a woman measure other women and a man for other men.

After Esmerelda was done, we left the boutique and headed back to the Big Stakes Casino. As we arrived, we called Carlo so we could go over a plan, but he never answered.

I told Evelyn, "I'm going to head to my room and relax. Once I hear from the tailor, I'll call you to let you know when it is done."

Before I could enter the lobby, Evelyn grabbed my arm and said, "How about we wait for the tailor in your room? Then we can head back to see Ezzy after you finish trying on your suit."

I took a deep breath, exhaled, and rubbed my head. Evelyn saw I was getting frustrated and said, "You need to relax for a bit. Why don't we just cuddle up, and that's it. My presence could help your mood some."

Evelyn grabbed my hand and said, "Come on, let's head up."

I gave in and walked with Evelyn. In my mind, I thought it was a bad idea, and I just wanted to sit back and relax. I know she's doing whatever she can to be with me.

What if I can't be that person she needs? My mind isn't all there yet for me to make choices like this. I feel comfortable around her, so maybe it is a start in a good direction.

We arrived at my room, and I plopped face-first onto the bed. The excellent cozy mattress felt so good to lay down on.

I turned onto my back, and I looked at Evelyn. I yelled, "What are you doing?!"

She was stripped down to her lingerie, standing at the end of the bed.

Evelyn responded, "I'm getting comfortable; now, move over so I can lay with you."

I threw my hands up in the air as she lay down on the bed with me. She threw her leg over my body, arms around my stomach, and her head onto my chest. As she did back at the house in Texas. She then started rubbing my chest.

I brought my hands down from being in the air. One hand was on Evelyn's back, and the other was on her arm around me. I caressed her soft skin as she lay there and saw her slowly moving and expressing small moans.

Evelyn said, "You know, all we are supposed to be doing is cuddling together. The way you're caressing me, you will get more than that."

As we lay in bed, my mind started returning to the first time Evelyn and I met. I couldn't help but notice how gorgeous she was in the red dress and what she told me as I stared.

While reminiscing the memory, I had a big smile and said aloud, "Damn."

Evelyn stopped rubbing my chest and said, "Huh? Why did you say damn for?"

"I was just thinking, and it slipped out."

"What were you thinking about that made you say that?"

"I can't believe how much we both changed from the first time we met. That was the reason why I said that. How our partnership and friendship developed over time into what it is now."

Evelyn snickered and rested her head back on my chest. She rubbed my chest again and said, "I'm just waiting for you to tell me I was right."

I replied, "What do you mean?"

"The night of the event, Carlo, you, and I went to the restaurant. I sat next to you and told you I could show you how comfortable you could become with me. Well, haven't you become comfy and cozy?"

She was correct; I have become more than serene being around her. I didn't think it was possible, but somehow and someway, she did it. There have been times that I thought of Karina and times that I forgot all about her.

"Hmm, too stubborn to admit it, huh?" Evelyn said.

I replied, "What?! No, I'm not stubborn to admit it. Yes, you are absolutely right; I have become satisfied with your presence around me."

Evelyn held me tighter, then asked, "I told you about my early life. What about your life when you were younger? What was it like for you growing up?"

"Well, as far as I can remember, I was a nerd growing up," I answered. "I had the latest toys that came out. With my dad always working at the foundry, we always had money saved up for extra stuff. My mom would make a decent amount but nothing compared to what my father brought home.

"I remember going to an all-boys school and always being first in my class, and I had all the answers for each subject I was in.

"I wasn't interested in dating or anything back then, and I wanted to prove that I could exceed better than what I did the prior year. My parents knew they didn't have to worry about leaving me alone since I never wanted to hang out with anyone. It was either reading or playing my video games.

"I had graduated high school summa cum laude, and I wanted to go to Harvard, but that's when I found Karina, and she didn't want me to leave her side. So I stayed back, and we moved to Kingman."

Did I just tell her my life story? Maybe I am becoming comfortable with her around. Is this a good thing or a bad thing, Will?

Evelyn replied, "Wow, I did not know that about you. Did your parents ever get mad at you for not seeking out your career with that high of honors?"

I laughed and said, "My dad was understanding about my choice. He saw the look in my eyes when I first met Karina, and he knew that I had found the one. On the other hand, my mom was irate that I didn't pursue a career. Eventually, she came around and became happy with my choice."

"So, are you a momma's boy or a daddy's boy?"

I snickered and said, "My dad was a big influence in my life, but my mom was always there for me, doing little things at school and always being around. It's hard to say which one I am because I looked to my dad as a mentor or idol. And the gentle, loving care from my mom was pure comfort."

Evelyn took a deep breath and said, "Do you want to know the real reason why I don't like the word honey?"

"I thought that was the real reason."

"My mom would call me that when I was younger. Every time I hear you call me that, it reminds me of her and I want to cry because I miss her."

I heard my phone going off on the nightstand as we lay there. It was from a number I didn't recognize, so I answered, "Hello."

"Hey Will, this is your tailor. I am heading upstairs with your suit right now, "The tailor replied.

I said, "Sounds good; Evelyn and I are here. Just knock when you are at the door."

After I hung up the phone, Evelyn received a call from Esmeralda about her dress being ready. Evelyn put some clothes on, and we awaited the tailor to arrive.

After the tailor delivered my suit and I tried it on, we headed out to the boutique.

We arrived back at the boutique, and Evelyn said to me, "Wait right here while I try it on."

I told myself, she gets to watch me dress, and I have to sit out here and wait for her. Women, I tell you, you will never understand them.

She walked out from the curtain in a gorgeous shimmering blue dress, which fit nicely all around her. My jaw dropped every second I looked at her.

"Well, how do I look," Evelyn asked.

I was so busy looking at her dress that I didn't even recognize she asked me something. My eyes were uncontrollable, moving from her bosom to her legs protruding from the sides.

"Will!" Evelyn exclaimed as she put her hands on her hips.

Still thinking in my head as I gaze at Evelyn in the dress, I had never seen Evelyn in such an elegant dress as this one. This lady is drop-dead gorgeous.

Evelyn walked over to me, placed her hands on my legs, and yelled, "Hey, I asked you a question! From your expression, I think I got my answer."

I stuttered, "I'm sorry, the dress astonished me,"

Evelyn smiled and reached in to kiss my cheek. I continued, "That is the most elegant and most beautiful dress I saw on you."

Evelyn stands in front of me, biting her lip, and intimately drags her nails on my legs. She then says, "I've been holding back whenever we are together, but tonight-." Evelyn leaned forward and takes an arousing heavy breath in my ear. "I am letting loose on you."

My eyes became big; what if I am not ready? So many things went through my mind as she said that. As we gazed into each other's eyes, my phone began to ring. I think it is safe to say I was saved by the ring from my phone.

I looked to see who it was and Carlo was calling. I answered, "Hey, boss."

Still close to my ear, Evelyn whispered, "You are lucky you were saved by Carlo."

Carlo replied, "I didn't interrupt a serious business altercation, did I?"

I said, "No, we were just—."

Before I could finish my sentence. Evelyn turns around with her back facing me and lifts her dress to expose her butt in front of me.

I continued to say slowly to Carlo, "Um, we were just, um... wow."

Carlo slowly responds, "How about I call you guys back in a bit."

"No, no, what's up, boss," I said. "We were finishing up at the boutique, ensuring everything fits before we head out tonight."

Carlo replies, "And from the tone in your voice, I take it the dress was a perfect fit? Hey, before I forget why I called you. I wanted to apologize for not answering earlier. I know we were supposed to go over plans, but something came up. Make sure to see Frank as soon as you get to the casino. He will be awaiting your arrival, and I told him you should be there around ten tonight. I can call him back and tell him a later time if you need me to."

I responded, "No, ten, ten is perfect. I will reach out to you once we leave."

Carlo humorously says, "Okay, be safe out there, and I mean both the casino and the boutique."

After the conversation, I looked at Evelyn and said, "Okay, the dress fits, and my suit fits. Carlo wants us to be out at the casino by ten. We have four hours before ten; I want to get a nap in before our long night. So how about we head back to the casino and let me take a nap. Whatever you have to do, go, and do and meet back at the casino by nine thirtyish. Sound good?"

Evelyn looks up at the ceiling, lets out a deep exhale, and says, "Fine! Even though you have me all aroused right now. I will have to wait until after we are done to have my fun."

I closed my eyes and said to myself, thank god. We made our way back to the casino.

After I went upstairs and took my nap, I woke up around eight-thirty and started to get ready. As I was just about to jump in the shower, I heard a knock on the door. All I had was my underwear on when I went to see who it was, and Evelyn was standing there holding her dress.

She looked at me and alluringly said, "Oh, nice to see the both of you."

I knew what she would ask before opening her mouth, so I said, "Yes, you can get ready here. I am about to jump in the shower and get ready myself."

Evelyn snickered and said, "Thanks, you're so good to me." She puts her hand on my face and grabs my cheek.

After I turned around, I felt a smack on my butt. I turned around with a startled look, rubbed where Evelyn just hit, and said, "Oww! What was that for? That hurt! That was almost bare cheek!"

"Oh, you liked it," Evelyn flirtatiously responded. "Hurry up and get ready. We don't have much time."

Once we got ready, we had a driver take us to the underground casino. I still can't get over how dark and creepy the walk is to get to the door. We arrived at the entrance and knocked on the door.

The sliding window opens, and a voice says, "Who are you? What business do you have here?"

I replied, "Will Bigsley, I am here to see Frank."

The window closes, and the door opens. A man behind the door says, "Frank is expecting you and the misses. Please, right this way."

We were brought to the office that frank was sitting in, and he said, "It is good to see you again, Will. How is everything going since our last meeting?

I replied, "Good, sir."

Frank turns to Evelyn, grabs her hand, and says, "The glamorous Evelyn, it has been a while since I bask in your presence. The both of you look great together."

He lets go of Evelyn's hand, looks at us both, and says, "Now, Carlo tells me what he wants to accomplish today. I am not too pleased to hear his motives for bringing you both here in this fashion. This is how we will arrange for this to happen. I will give you money from the safe and use it as you please. Sit at tables or next to others at the slots. But do not, and I mean DO NOT, disrupt the flow of my casino. Are we clear?"

We both nodded our heads and headed out to the casino floor. Evelyn followed me, and we stopped by a wall to scope the ambience.

Evelyn asked, "Do you know how to play card games?"

"I know five-card poker, but that's it," I answered.

"This may be a problem; let's walk around for a bit," Evelyn said.

We stopped at a table with the name CRAPS on the screen. There were about 12 people around the table, and I said to Evelyn, "Let's start here."

As we moved closer to the table, something told me to look up, and I noticed Frank talking to a couple of security guards pointing toward us. Frank then walked over to another set of guards and did the same thing.

I nudged Evelyn and whispered, "Frank is talking to guards and pointing our way. I feel like something is wrong."

Evelyn replied, "Good eye, let's step back from the table and rethink our motive."

Two guards came over to us, and one said, "Frank needs to talk to you. It is urgent."

We walked with the guards back to Frank's office, and I asked Frank, "What's going on?"

Frank hands me a phone, and Carlo is on the other end. Carlo says, "End your task and come back. Come see me tomorrow morning. Tell Evelyn I need to see her asap!"

He hung up the phone, and I handed it back to Frank. I turned to Evelyn and said, "Carlo needs us to end our task and come back. He wants me to see him tomorrow morning, but he wants to see you asap when we get back."

Evelyn turns to Frank and says, "Well, thank you, Frank, for allowing us to conduct our mission."

I handed Frank the money he gave me, and I shook his hand, then Evelyn and I left the casino. We got into the vehicle, and the driver took us back to Big Stakes Casino.

After we arrived, we both entered the lobby. Evelyn gave me a kiss and said, "See you tomorrow morning. Get a good night's sleep."

She walked away into a hallway, and I headed upstairs to get some sleep. I got undressed and fell onto the bed. I turned over onto my back and stared at the ceiling. The one question that kept popping up as these events unfolded was, what did I get myself into? I knew for sure I didn't know how to answer that question. Was I eventually going to be able to answer it?

Chapter 10

Early the next day, I woke up and looked out the window. I said to myself, I feel like today will be a good day. After I got ready, I headed downstairs to see Carlo. The one thing on my mind was, why did Carlo suddenly stop us? Something must have happened for Carlo to call off the task like that. I left my room, went to the lobby, and saw Carlo and Evelyn waiting patiently for me.

I looked at Carlo and Evelyn and said, "Good morning, so what is this all about?"

Carlo replied, "We received a special package last night, and it made me smile as soon as I heard about it."

"What is it?"

"It's like Christmas time, and it's not even close to opening any presents yet. Come, follow me and I will show you."

I followed Carlo and Evelyn downstairs into a dark hallway. The lights were motion detectors, so the lights would turn on every couple of steps we took.

We came to a door that three security guards were guarding. Carlo whispered something to the guard in the middle, and then that guard whispered something to the other two guards.

I thought to myself, what is going on here?

I looked over at Evelyn, leaned in, and whispered in her ear, "If they're whispering about something, then I'll whisper something to you too."

She had a serious look as she turned toward me. Then sent a jab that went right for my side. I jumped but held in my scream so we didn't look suspicious.

Evelyn then said to me, "Behave!"

Carlo looked back at us and said, "You guys playing touchy-touchy back there?"

Evelyn rolled her eyes and said, "No, he's acting childish."

I said to Evelyn, "I am not!"

Carlo turned around and said, "Whatever it is, you guys need to calm down!"

We both became scared because we looked straight to the floor once Carlo said that. I was trying to have a little fun in this rigorous moment.

Carlo turned back around, and the guards opened the door for us to enter. In the room, a man was hanging from the ceiling with his hands tied behind his back. Next to him was a guy using a whip to hit him and another guy on the opposite side asking him questions. I thought these places only existed in the movies or make-believe stuff.

The questions I heard the guy asking the tied-up man were, "Who sent you? Why are you here? Do you know whose casino you entered and snooping around?"

Carlo tells the guy asking questions, "Take a break."

Then Carlo tells the guy with the whip, "Give this to the man back there." As he points in my direction.

What am I to do with this? Does he expect me to hit this guy to leak some intel out? Okay, Will, stay calm, just stay calm. Keep your composure; you can do this.

The guy with the whip walks over to me and hands me the whip. I looked at it; it has pointy spikes going down the whip. I said to myself, these got to hurt.

Carlo said to me with a smile while he rubbed his hands together, "Let's get your hands dirty."

Evelyn reaches over and touches my shoulder before I walk over to Carlo. She then says seductively, "Don't worry, I have one of those too. We can try it out later in the bedroom since I still haven't had my fun yet."

I looked at her with a confused face. I thought she just told ME to behave. Who just says that? I don't want no one whipping me, especially with something that looks like it's from medieval times. What does that even mean anyway? Why would someone want to be hit with a whip in the first place? That is without question something you should not bring to the bedroom.

I shook my head and headed over to Carlo. He said, "Stand over there, and I'll be right here asking questions."

The tied-up guy told Carlo, "Is it bring your kids to work day?"

Carlo looked at the guy and used the back of his hand to smack the heck out of him. The smack echoed so loud that the sound rang forever in the walls. My jaw dropped when I felt the vibration from that smack.

I turned to look at Evelyn; she was standing there with her arms crossed as if she'd seen something like this. I'm sure she probably has since she has been working with Carlo.

Carlo yelled out to me, "Are you paying attention!"

I turned back to look at Carlo.

He said to the guy, "Now I'm going to ask you some questions. If I don't like what I hear, he will slay that whip into your back. What is the reason for you being here?"

The guy said to Carlo, "Like I told the other numb nut that asked me the same question. I am just a guy enjoying some casino time while I was out and about. What is it with you people? Think your all-tough guy, badass because you have someone tied up? You are just as stupid as the next guy to come and interrogate me."

The guy hacks up some spit and shoots it at Carlo.

I grabbed that whip without hesitation and laid every bit of those spikes into that man's back. The snap was as loud, if not louder, than the smack Carlo hit him with.

The scream that the guy let out was a cry of agony. Did I just do that? Did I just use every ounce of my muscles to dig those spikes and leather of the whip against his bare skin?

I was more impressed with myself than Carlo because I initiated that hit without him telling me.

Carlo said to the guy again, "I'm going to ask you one more time. You saw my guy's power, and he's not afraid to use it."

As he said that to the guy. I thought in my head, I was afraid to use it, but that was instinct once I saw the guy spit at Carlo.

Carlo told the guy, "I know who you are, and your loyalty lies with Antonio, right?"

The guy hesitated before saying, "I do not know who this Antonio guy is that you just named. I know plenty of guys with that name, but I don't have a reason or anything to create loyalty for someone with that name. Like I said, I am just a gambler trying to have some fun here."

Evelyn walks up to the guy, places her hand on his chest, and enticingly says, "All we are asking is if you can cooperate with us for a moment. Then we will cut you loose, and you'll be free. Now you wouldn't want to keep a darling like me waiting, would you?"

As she said that, she removed her hand from the guy's chest and started rubbing every inch of her body in front of this guy.

Even caught my attention while she was swaying from right to left with her hips. I'm not even the one getting interrogated, and I wanted to confess what I've been hiding.

The guy says to Evelyn, "Um... um... miss, I am... I'm telling the god-forsaken truth. I don't know anything about no other casino or anything."

Evelyn gets closer to the guy, places a finger on his chin, and seductively says, "Well, that's too bad you don't know anything. I would take it easy on you, unlike these boys and their muscles. Pleasure gets me what I want, and right now, I just want you to talk to me and tell me about this other casino. I'll see to it and try to let you go free."

The guy says to Evelyn, "If I talk, he will kill me."

Evelyn provocatively replied, "Who will kill you, sweety? Maybe I can help you?"

The guy answered, "*Antonio.*"

Evelyn responded, "Can you speak up louder. I couldn't understand you." She rubbed and pushed up on her breasts as she continued in a teasing tone, "If you want alllllllll of this, then cooperate."

The guy replied, "Antonio!"

Evelyn looked at him with a satisfying smirk, a similar one she gave me as we were in the shower, and said, "Thank you. You have been more than accommodating today." Then walks away into the shadows and disappears.

I am still shocked that she got all that out of this man using her womanly wiles.

Did I just fall in love with Evelyn? No, stop that right now. Get your head back into the game and focus on what's at hand in front of you.

Carlo said to the guy, "See how easy that was. Less painful than the whip, and you were cooperative. Now, why did Antonio send you here?"

The guy looked around the room for Evelyn and then said to Carlo, "I thought she was going to let me go."

"She'll try to see about letting you go free. I still need some answers from you. So, you are not going anywhere until I say so."

The guy said to Carlo and me, "Woman, you got to love them, right? I think that was more painful than the whip slaps. I should have known it was too good to be true. Out of desperation, you guys sent in the secret weapon against a man. Even for me, that's a low blow."

Carlo responded to the guy, "That is right, you got to love them. Can I get these answers so we can be on our way? And, if you're lucky, I'll let you leave here freely."

The guy went quiet for a moment. The rope rubbing against the rafters in the ceiling was starting to get louder and louder as no one was talking anymore.

Should I initiate one more whip snap to get this guy going again?

I gripped the whip tighter, and Carlo looked at me and shook his head no. I released my grip, and Carlo said to the guy, "So, what will it be?"

The guy took a deep breath and said, "There have been talks of Antonio taking over this strip. He has been targeting your casino and strip club. Since you are a very wealthy man, he can't just rush in like a bull. He's sitting back, waiting for the perfect chance to make his move. He sent me here to do some surveillance on you, then report what I saw back to Antonio."

Carlo started to rub his chin as he heard the confession from the man. The look on Carlo's face seemed as if he was in a deep train of thought. Maybe processing everything through to make sense out of it all.

Carlo then grabbed a knife from the table behind him.

The guy seemed very nervous and yelled, "Wait, I told you everything I know. That must account for something, right?"

Holding the knife tightly and thinking deeply, Carlo grabs the rope and slices through it. The guy drops to the floor; Carlo then cuts the rope from his tied hands.

He then tells the guy, "I am being very generous right now. Don't make me change my mind, get outta here."

The guy runs off through the room entrance and disappears into the shadows. I looked at Carlo and asked, "Is this a good idea to let him go like that?"

Carlo placed the knife back on the table and stood there momentarily. I felt there was some doubt in his choice, but what is done is done.

"I'm going to send you and Evelyn on a mission in a couple of days," Carlo said. "We will send a message that will hopefully distance ourselves from having to create another war over this situation."

I said to myself, another? What does he mean by another? Has he had trouble in the past with this Antonio guy?

I told Carlo, "Okay, let's make sure this is what should be done, though. I don't want to see you fail, boss, and I am sure not going to let you do that while I'm working for you."

Carlo turned around and started to walk toward me. He stops next to me, places his hand on my shoulder, and says, "That's why I signed you up as my right-hand man, and I knew I could count on your loyalty."

He then walks out of the room and disappears into the shadows also. I stood there with this spiked whip, still wondering what had just happened.

Then I asked myself, was that feeling true about Evelyn when I saw her working with the guy? Is this fate running its course and sending me to her? She has been there for me ever since Karina left, and not once had she left my side. I know we were working jobs together, but something is definitely there.

Should I invite her over tonight for dinner or something? I took a deep breath and exhaled with a sigh.

I headed for the door and went up the stairs back into the casino lobby. I didn't see Carlo or Evelyn, so I returned to the hotel room. I grabbed my clothes and all my stuff. I headed for the lobby, gave the main desk my room keys, and jumped into my vehicle. Then, headed home to clean up a little.

I got home and opened the door to quietness again. A place that I used to call home does not feel like home anymore. A small glimpse of memories runs through my mind as I walk into each room. I see Ashley playing with her toys in her room, then I see Karina in our room, lying on the bed, waiting for me to come to join her. I head to the kitchen and see Karina making meals for us as I get home from work.

The dealership, I haven't checked on the place in a while. Carlo lent me a guy to do some selling for me as I am gone. Lately, I have been neglecting my business.

I got back into my vehicle and headed to the dealership. All the lights were off; it wasn't even around closing time. Maybe business isn't that good since I've been gone. I need to check in more often, perhaps tomorrow, since I don't have anything to do for the next couple of days.

I got back into my car, grabbed my phone, and searched for Evelyn's name. I hesitated to press the call button for about twenty minutes. I finally built up enough courage to press the call button. It rang twice until she picked up.

Evelyn answered, "Hey, handsome."

I became very nervous and didn't know what to say. My breathing got heavier and deeper each second went by. My hands were shaking, and I was sweating profusely.

Evelyn said with a worried tone, "Is everything alright, Will? You are scaring me, and it isn't funny. Speak, burp, or do something so I know you're there."

I finally got the courage to speak and said, "I'm sorry, I am nervous right now and didn't know what to say. I need to ask you something, but I don't know if I'll be able to get it out. So, if you could be patient with me so I can ask you, that would be great."

"I am so sorry for laughing, but this is cute hearing how nervous you are. Where are you at right now?"

"I came to the dealership to check in on the guy Carlo lent me, but no one is here. So, now I think I will head home and just relax there. My question is, would you like to come over for dinner? I'm not a great cook, but some company would be good tonight."

Evelyn paused briefly before saying, "Oh my god, you just asked me over to your house. I feel like our relationship is starting to go in the right direction. I just got out of the shower like thirty minutes ago. So, give me some time to get ready, and I'll be right over."

I had to think for a second; she never asked me for my address or where do I live. So, I asked her, "Do you need my address or describe my house."

Evelyn replied, "Well... you see when Karina was around, the boss and I kept tags on you and the family. We would come to the area, sit back, and watch as time passed. Once Karina left, and you agreed to join us, I stopped coming around."

My heart raced through my chest; my mind went silent. How did I now just learn of all this happening?

My feeling went from confused to irate within seconds. I started to breathe faster, and I developed a headache that ran from the front of my brain to the back.

Evelyn said, "I am sorry, don't be mad. How about we reschedule this session, and I'll come over another day?"

I returned to reality and quickly said, "No, I'm okay. I wasn't prepared to hear any of that, that's all. Come over, please, and we'll keep our conversations going. I am sure a little fun is what I need right now also."

Evelyn laughed and replied, "Now you're speaking my language. I am about to leave the casino. So, I'll see you in a bit." Then she hung up the phone.

I sat in my vehicle, still holding my phone up to my ear as if she was on the other side. I took a deep gulp and thought, is this really happening? Did I really ask her to come over? Am I going to regret this action? I grabbed my keys, started my vehicle, and headed home.

On the drive home, all I could think of was what happened in the hotel room. Is it because I'm lonely I need someone to be there with me? Do I need a person's physical presence to feel better? What will happen once I get that presence and scare my mind away?

I pulled into my driveway, walked inside, and started cleaning up around the house. Of course, it looks like a man's home with no woman living here. Is that even attractive for a woman to see?

I finished everything around the house and thought to myself, food! What am I going to make for us? I invited her over to eat, and all there was made was air.

I am a hot mess right now. I hear a knocking on the door. Shit, there's no food made yet. Has the time gone by that quick? Did Evelyn drive fast to beat the time when I said the word fun?

I walked over to the door and opened it.

Evelyn looked gorgeous as ever as she stood there in front of me.

"Well, are you going to invite me in?" Evelyn said. Then she started rubbing down her curves as she did while we interrogated the guy and said, "Or just let me stand here so you can admire all this glamor."

I said, "No, I... I... I mean, yes, come in. Please, make yourself at home."

Evelyn approached me and whispered, "Make myself at home? So, are you insinuating that this will be my new home?"

She nibbled on my ear and walked to the kitchen after saying that.

I had to catch my breath after she hit me with her irresistible passion. I closed the door, turned around to see where she went, and she was looking at me while in the kitchen.

I said to her, "I am sorry. The time flew by, and before I knew it, you were knocking on the door, and dinner wasn't even decided yet.

"Oh lord, you definitely need a woman's touch around here," Evelyn said as she laughed. "Maybe I should take your offer then."

Evelyn walked around looking in my cabinets, cupboards, and my pantry. She then said, "You need a woman's touch and groceries. How do men even survive with stuff like this? I would have died by starvation by now if this was me."

I made my way to where Evelyn was, grabbed her hands, and said, "Earlier, when you were talking to the guy. I saw a different person than what I normally see from you. I think it's time I just say what is on my mind."

Evelyn's eyes got big, but she also had a confused face.

She then replied, "Will, are you okay? This isn't the normal Will that I see daily either. What is going on here? You're not dying on me, are you? I don't want to be a widow at such a young age."

Still holding her hands, I hung my head in shame.

Then I laughed and said, "No, I am not dying. And technically, we must be married for you to become a widow. I wanted to let go of my feelings and tell you everything."

Evelyn began gripping my hand tighter, looked up at me, and reached her head for a kiss.

Here we go, the moment that made everything go insane in the hotel room. Do I kiss Evelyn back? Or do I tell her not yet? I gave in and kissed her lips.

She let go of my hands, wrapped her arms around my neck, and pulled me closer. Even though that night was a nightmare, I still love kissing her soft lips. It feels like a piece of heaven every time we kiss each other.

I don't want this moment to end; I want it to go on forever.

As we kissed each other, I heard a knocking on the door. I released my lips from hers and asked Evelyn, "Are you expecting someone else to join us? Did you tell Carlo to meet us here?"

Looking confused, Evelyn said, "No, this is your place. You must be awaiting guests."

I walked over to the door, and I could feel Evelyn behind me. I looked back and said, "Why are you sneaking up on me?"

Evelyn replied, "I'm not; I have your back if anything goes wrong. That is what a real woman does."

I shook my head and turned my attention to the door. I slowly creaked it open; no one was out there. I looked around outside, and no one was standing there.

I told Evelyn, "What the heck? There's no one."

I turned to face Evelyn, slowly started closing the door, and said, "Now, where were we."

I could feel something stop the door as it almost shut. I turned my attention to the door, and Evelyn said, "What is it?"

A force blew the door wide open. Evelyn and I hit the floor hard.

Two guys entered the house and threw a bag over my head.

I could hear Evelyn screaming and shouting, "Get this thing off my head!"

I tried fighting the guys, but I could not see anything.

Then I hear Evelyn calling to me, "Will, Will! Get off me! Are you okay, Will?"

I told Evelyn, "They have my hands tied together, and I can't see a god damn thing."

Then suddenly, I received a blow to my stomach that made me scream and fall to the ground.

"Will, what happened?" Evelyn yelled out. Suddenly, I heard her scream as loud as I did.

I yelled out, "Evelyn! Don't you lay another finger on her!"

Then someone grabbed me and dragged me out of my house and into what felt like a van.

From inside this place, I could hear Evelyn crying, "Will! Will! NO!"

Then I heard a loud gunshot. BANG!

I don't hear her calling me anymore. It is hushed, and that bang could only mean one thing. I yelled out, "You bastards!"

I heard the doors inside the cab open; two men entered and then closed the doors. I hear the footsteps getting into the van and a door closing.

I yelled out again, crying, "Where…. Is… Evelyn!? What… did… you do… with her!?"

A deep voice said to me, "Don't you worry. Evelyn is being well taken care of right now."

I feel the van moving, and the same voice says to me, "The same is going for you. You are going night-night." A hard blow to my head knocks me out cold.

Chapter 11

I opened my eyes to a dark room. I could not see anything or anyone around me. I couldn't move as my arms were still tied behind my back. I saw Carlo walking towards me from a distance, and Evelyn was walking alongside him.

Carlo arrived before me and stuck his hand out for a handshake, and I couldn't even shake his hand with my arms tied behind my back. I looked down, and somehow my hands were free from the shackles. I did a complete 360 spin, and I didn't see anything that held my hands together. Carlo stood there with his hand out, awaiting me to shake it.

As I shook his hand, he said, "You must be the infamous Will I hear so much about. My name is Carlo, and this beautiful lady is Evelyn."

I said to Carlo, "What's with the introduction? You already know who I am, Carlo. It's me, Will!"

Carlo and Evelyn walked away into the darkness and faded away.

What was that all about? I was so confused about what was going on. I shook his hand, and it felt like it was his hand.

I see a streetlight turn on in the corner of my eye.

Then a building with a bunch of lights came about in the background with the name 'Ocean's Paradise.' This is the strip club I went to when I decided to join Carlo.

I approached the doors and pushed them open. I entered and didn't see anyone in sight, but I heard music playing in the background. That same music was playing when I first walked into the club. There were no bouncers, no security whatsoever around.

I remembered where Carlo's table was and made my way over there. I saw him sitting there by himself with just a glass half full. I walked up to him and said, "Carlo! It's me, Will. What is going on? You keep showing up and then fading away into the darkness.

Carlo looked up at me and said, "Sit; you're making me nervous just standing there."

Behind me, I felt a hand touch my shoulder. I looked back, and Evelyn came walking by with five other ladies. I couldn't take my eyes off Evelyn as she walked past me. My eyes teared up. I reached out for her, but as I touched her, she faded away.

She reappeared on the couch next to Carlo, wearing the same elegant dress she had that day. I sat down in the chair and made myself comfortable.

Carlo then placed his hand on Evelyn's lap and said, "Do you remember Evelyn?"

She gave me that same enticing wave as she did before. Then, Evelyn got up, walked toward me, and sat on my lap. I reached out for her again, and she faded away.

I looked over at Carlo, and he said, "This life is not easy. You play the table with the hand you are dealt with, and it's on you whether you want to fold it in or make some use of it."

He then fades away along with the table and club.

There I was again, standing alone in the dark. No one to talk to or tell me what is happening. I looked up and let out a huge scream, arghhhhh!

I hear a voice behind me in the distance. It sounded like a familiar voice, but I couldn't determine who it was.

I turned around and saw another streetlight flickering on and off this time. I walked over to the light and saw Blake sitting at his desk.

He got up from his chair, walked over to me, and said, "Hello, I am Blake Fenningway, and this is my dealership. I read your application and think you would be a perfect fit for this place. Especially for what I have in store for the future. What do you say? Would you like to join my crusade and take over the world?"

He then faded away into the darkness like everyone else.

What in the world is going on? Why am I reminiscing on all these memories?

I saw a streetlight in the distance turn on, then another, and then a long line of them turned on simultaneously. I saw a set of headlights coming right towards me. It looked like a semi-moving pretty fast approaching me. I tried moving, but my legs wouldn't budge. I braced for impact the closer it became. The headlights appeared brighter and more intense until I saw the dark room clear up into a white room.

I felt a pain in my head; it felt like a headache. The pain kept getting more robust and heavier until I dropped to the floor in pain.

Screaming in agony, I closed my eyes to see if the pain would disappear. Then I opened my eyes and was in a room, tied up and sitting on the floor. I looked around to see where I was and could not determine the place.

I tried moving my arms and hands, but the rope they used was too tight to try and wiggle out of. My legs were also tied together, and there was no getting out of this one.

Who would do this?

Why would someone go that far to get me out of my house?

Evelyn? Where is she? Just when I became happy with life, it took a nosedive and crumbled. I hope she is okay, maybe Carlo will help me escape.

Suddenly, I saw a door swing wide open, and three people with masks walked in. There was a presence of a person behind them, but I couldn't make out what that person looked like.

The lights turned on inside the room, and I was blinded by how fast they turned on. I closed my eyes so my headache wouldn't worsen with the light's shine.

I heard footsteps approaching me, and I was picked up from the floor. I opened my eyes, and the three men were standing me up and hanging a harness onto me from the ceiling.

Oh great, now I feel like the guy Carlo had in that room hanging.

Wait a minute! I think the light bulb turned on above my head. What was the name that the guy said?

One of the guys cut the rope with my arms and hands tied. They placed the harness around my upper body and locked it around my waist. Then they cut the cord around my legs and finished the harness locking from under my groin. They pulled me up so I could hang by a harness in the ceiling. I thought to myself, this harness hurts. They couldn't move the straps to the side and away from my balls.

I started squirming like a worm, but it was no use. I wasn't going to go anywhere with this thing around me.

Then the presence of a person came forward in front of me. The person was an older gentleman, who looked like an older, maybe a Russian man.

I hear the older man say with a strong accent, "Stop moving!"

Then punched me in the gut, knocking all the wind out of me. The only thing I could do was just sway back and forth from the power of the punch. I tried to speak, but I was only gasping for air. That accent, he definitely sounded Russian, I thought.

Finally, I was able to recover my breath. I took a couple deep breaths and asked the older gentleman, "Who are you guys? Where am I? What about Evelyn? Where is she?"

"You talk too much," the older man said as he hit me again in the same spot. There I was, gasping for air again from the hit.

What did I do to deserve this?

I noticed another person walking in through the door. As he entered, everyone stepped aside as if he was someone essential. He looked at the older Russian and said, "That will be enough. Thank you."

His voice almost sounded similar to Carlo's, but I knew it wasn't him.

The Russian guy replied, "Of course, Antonio."

That was the name of the guy that I was trying to think of. Oh no, if that's the case, I'm about to be interrogated like we did the one guy.

Please don't hit me with a spiked whip; I don't think I could take that much pain.

Antonio walks up to me, puts his hand under my chin to lift my head, and says, "So you are the right-hand, huh? It's a pleasure to make your acquaintance. My name is Antonio.

"I heard from a little birdy what you did to one of my men. I should be thanking Carlo, actually. He exposed one of my weakest links inside my organization, and I can't have any weaklings here.

"So, I disposed of him, and now I have something better than what Carlo had. His right-hand man and woman. Christmas and my birthday came early this year."

I said to Antonio, "What did you do with Evelyn? Where is she?"

Antonio laughed and replied, "The blushing bride-to-be. I thought you guys had something going on, but I wasn't sure. It crossed my mind when my men told me who they picked up, and I wasn't going to ask questions. Honestly, it's none of my business. Now that you mentioned it, though, I may have something for you."

I hung there with a confused look on my face. I thought to myself, I need to stay quiet from now on. I'm saying too much for Antonio to use against me.

Where are you at, Carlo? Please, save me from this mess.

Antonio said to me, "The turtle hides in his shell once he is exposed to ravaging predators. I'm just going to be blunt with you. I do not need a right-hand man as mine would never get caught in a predicament like this. But I have some room on my team for someone with your knowledge, determination, and persistence."

I cannot believe this guy offered me a job on his team even though I am loyal to Carlo. He must be out of his mind to ask me such a question. There is no way that I would work for him, let alone leave Carlo's team. He started me in all of this; without him, I wouldn't have the knowledge I do.

I told Antonio, "I will have to decline your offer, but thanks anyway. I am loyal to Carlo and would never leave his side for anything."

Antonio let out a long, deep laugh and said, "I was hoping you would say something like that. Before asking something like this, I had to do my homework. Being part of Carlo's team, you lost your girlfriend and daughter. That's mighty big for someone like you.

"Your boss was shot dead right in front of you, and I am sure that wound is still freshly new, right? In the assignment you were sent on, your partner was shot. You don't have too many people left for me to threaten you except-."

He let out a malevolent cackle and added, "Your dreamy new damsel."

I became irate and furious with this man. I started moving around in the harness to try and set myself free. Nothing still wasn't working. I need to get free to save Evelyn and knock some sense into this idiot.

The more I struggled, it seemed as if I was making the harness tighter.

Antonio then grabbed me by the shoulders to stop me from moving. He smiled in my face and asked, "So, what'll it be? Will I add another member to my staff or dispose of you?"

I replied, "Let me see Evelyn first to ensure she is safe! Then I'll decide what I'm going to do."

Antonio rubbed his chin to think and said, "Hmm, what an attractive offer you're throwing down on the table. But I am declining the offer and giving you one more chance to give me the answer I want."

What will Evelyn think if I say yes to this bastard, and we won't be able to see each other anymore?

Carlo will be beyond pissed knowing I jumped ship and joined someone else, especially his competitor.

What do I do? What do I do?!

Antonio lifts his wrist to show a watch and says, "tick-tock, tick-tock, time is running out."

I yelled out, "Fine! I will join you but let me see Evelyn."

Antonio turns to his guys and says, "Bring him down, boys; we got ourselves a new hitter in the game."

The three masked people came over and undid the locks on the harness. My body falls to the floor and makes a loud thud sound.

I looked at them and said, "Thanks, you guys could have caught me."

Antonio turned around and faced the door; he walked towards it and stopped. He then says to the three masked people, "Bring her in for him."

The masked people left the room and carried Evelyn in, and threw her body to the ground hard. There were two gunshot wounds through her head. I felt her wrist for a pulse; she was colder than an ice cube.

I grabbed her face and yelled out, "Evelyn! No, no, no! Evelyn! Why?!"

I sat up, rested my back against the wall, and said, "Oh god, no! Oh god, Evelyn, NO!"

I yelled to Antonio, "You knew she was dead already but used her as bait to get me to join you. You are a sadistic person; why would you even do something like this?"

"You wanted to see Evelyn, and I granted your wish," Antonio said. "Oh, and by the way, your old phone is no more. I don't need you to contact anyone from the past, and my guys will get you a brand new one to use."

Antonio and his crew left the room.

I sat there on the floor gazing at Evelyn's body. I touched her face and cried, "I am sorry for all of this. I loved you and didn't even get a chance to tell you. I fought for us not to be together and ended up wanting you in my life. It's too late, and we can't even be together."

I closed her eyes, kissed her forehead, and said, "I love you!"

I got up from the floor and walked out of the room.

I don't even know my way around here. No tour guide to direct me to where I needed to go.

I kept on walking down a long hallway until I found some stairs. I went up the stairs and found myself in the kitchen.

I asked one of the cooks, "How do I get to the lobby from here?"

He gave me some directions, and I went to the lobby.

Awaiting me was Antonio by the counter. He said, "I was wondering how long it was going to take you to come up here and let me give you a proper showing around my casino."

He lifted one of his arms and said, "Welcome to The Enchanted Tomb Casino."

After his tour, he gave me my keys and said, "You can either stay here for a discounted price or stay at your place. Whatever you do is up to you, and I do have a task for you to do today. So, if you are going to head home, I would make sure to go right now and be back before sundown."

Before I left, I asked Antonio, "What will happen to my dealership?"

Antonio said as he laughed, "What Dealership? The place has always been owned by Carlo. Since he shot Fenningway dead, he left it in your hands to run, but that's it. It's probably closed down by now."

In frustration, I left the casino and headed home. I pulled into the driveway and noticed blood on the grass by the porch. I could not help but cry as I knew that was where they shot Evelyn.

My body started to shiver from a feeling of sadness. A couple of boards from the porch were missing, and the front door had one hinge off. I told myself I should just grab all my clothes and stay at the casino. I grabbed a duffle bag, shoved as many clothes as possible, and returned to the casino.

I walked in, and Antonio was by the front counter still. He saw my bag and said, "Smart choice."

He showed me to the room where I would be staying. The room was similar to the one I stayed at in Big Stakes casino.

I turned to Antonio and said, "Can I at least take a shower and get ready?"

He replied, "Make it fast."

After my shower, I got ready and headed downstairs to the lobby.

A guy in a trench coat walks up to me and whispers, "Take this envelope without looking suspicious."

I grabbed the envelope, and the guy walked away without me asking any questions. What am I supposed to do with this? I walked over to a table in the café, opened it, and it had a piece of paper.

It was a short note that read:

> *Call Jullian on the phone inside this envelope
> and have him bring a vehicle to take you to the
> airport. From there, wait for a man wearing a
> red and yellow shirt coming in from a flight.
> Follow him and make sure he does not live to
> see another day.*

I grabbed the phone and scrolled through the contacts. I found the name Jullian and gave him a call.

"Are you ready?" He asked as he answered the phone.

I replied, "Yes, I'm at the casino."

"Ten minutes, be outside!" He then hung the phone up

This guy means some serious business, I said to myself. Everything is so uptight over here. Carlo's operation was more flexible and fun.

I better not say that out loud and become a target. I looked at the phone; what time did I call Jullian? Has it been ten minutes already?

I headed outside to see if anyone was upfront. I didn't even ask what car he drives or anything. Actually, he didn't give me a chance to ask.

I started pacing back and forth by the entrance thinking this was not a good idea. I don't feel too comfortable doing this.

As I was doing all this, a luxurious sedan pulled up in front of me, and the guy said, "Get in!"

I got in the vehicle, and we took off. I have never been inside one of these before; this is nice. I rubbed the leather on the door; this feels amazing. Now I see why people love these vehicles.

Then, the guy said, "I'm Jullian; in the glove compartment is a gun. Conceal it at all times to not warn anyone that you got it. We only have one shot at doing this."

I nodded my head yes.

The whole ride to the airport was nothing but silence. No music, no talking, nothing. This man was on a different level than I am used to, and it seemed like he was a professional in this line of work.

We arrived at the airport and waited by the arriving door.

Jullian said, "He'll come through that door, and his flight will land in twenty minutes. Make sure you are ready for when we follow him."

Twenty-five minutes passed, and still no man in a red and yellow shirt.

I told Jullian, "Maybe he changed shirts and missed him that way."

He looked at me disgusted and said, "Don't be foolish; my intel has never been wrong. Just sit there, stay quiet, and be patient."

I wanted to say that the timing was off, but I figured I'd keep my mouth shut and pay attention outside.

Finally, a man with a red and yellow shirt came out.

Jullian sat correctly in his seat and said, "You better be ready, newbie. No mistakes."

The guy got into a vehicle and drove away. Jullian began to pursue him, and he had stayed at least 5 car lengths behind the other car.

Then he tapped my leg and said, "Get it ready; we are making a stop."

The vehicle pulled into a parking lot and dropped off the guy. I got out of the car and walked right up to him. I went to pull the gun out, and the guy quickly pulled a gun out on me before I could take the shot.

Now I'm in a situation I didn't want to be in. Out in the open, two guns are pointing at different people.

The guy says, "I knew he would send someone after me, and that man is so predictable. So, are you man enough to pull it? Are you able to cancel someone's lifeline in one shot?"

I stayed quiet and didn't want to give away anything. In my head, I was thinking about the time when Evelyn and I had our guns out together. Damn, I miss her being here with me.

A loud crash behind the guy made him divert his attention.

That's when I was able to pull the trigger and run back to the vehicle. Jullian shifted into reverse, drove, and got away from the scene.

As we went by, I looked at the guy's dead body on the pavement as it lay in a puddle of blood.

Jullian said to me in an infuriated tone, "You almost cost us the mission. You're an idiot for not taking the shot right away! What were you thinking?"

Evelyn, that was who I was thinking of, I said in my head. This was starting to become too much for me.

We arrived back at the casino, and Jullian said, "Leave the gun in the glove box and get out."

I hurried and got out of the vehicle. Jullian sped off and left.

My hand was still shaking from pulling the trigger. How do people feel good about pulling a trigger? I thought Evelyn said this feeling would go away. I need a drink, I said to myself.

I went to the bar and noticed a gorgeous lady standing at the counter.

Her hair was up in a bun, and her dress was a long, crème color that almost touched the floor. It had a slit on both sides to expose her legs. Diamond studs in her ears that shimmered so elegant.

I don't need to be checking anyone out at this moment in my life. What's really important is focusing on myself right now.

I walked up next to her and ordered a beer. The smell of her perfume left an everlasting impression on my nose, and I could stand there for hours with that fragrance. The aroma had a similar scent to what Evelyn would wear.

I shook my head to stay focused.

I grabbed my beer and was about to walk off when she asked me, "Well, aren't you going to offer to buy me something?"

I stopped in my tracks, turned around, and asked her, "What is your name?"

She smiled and replied, "Why do we need to know names if all you're going to do is buy me a drink?"

I paused, placed my hand on the counter next to her, and said, "Have a good day, ma'am."

Then walked away and went to sit down at a table.

As I sat at the table, I heard the TV above me saying, "Parlay bets are where it's at if you're looking to score some serious cash. Download the phone apps or visit your nearest casino for more details. You could turn your dollar into one hundred dollars."

I heard the word parlay and hung my head low. This is what caused the tragic events to unfold. Then I put my elbows on the table and held my head in frustration.

I looked up and noticed a couple TVs had some sports playing. I reminisced about the first time Blake took me to create my first bet.

Then I remembered what that guy told me at the 'Place Your Bets' building. He told me that first day, "Curiosity killed the cat."

Was all of this part of me satisfying my curiosity? If I had never stuck my nose into that place, Karina would still be here. Blake would still own the dealership, and Evelyn wouldn't have died for anything.

171

I sat there thinking about the what-ifs and what never would have happened.

Then I felt a hand on my shoulder that made me jump a little.

Antonio was behind me smiling and said, "Easy killer, it's only me."

He then took a seat in the chair across from me. He leaned back in the chair and said, "Jullian told me what happened. Now I can't have errors in this business, and that's how people become missing or simply MIA."

I looked at him and asked, "What is MIA?"

He laughed at me and said, "Missing in action." He leaned forward and said, "What if he would have pulled the trigger before you could do anything? You wouldn't be here right now, and I would be down a guy again.

"You must consider your actions and possibilities when doing this job. Be ready for outcomes, plan B, or, as a matter of fact, plan the rest of the alphabet. But ensure you are always ready to move in a millisecond."

I took a sip of my beer to wash down the nasty taste I had in my mouth from this conversation.

What do I tell Antonio? These words are coming into my head, but I am not saying anything.

Then I told him, "I'm sorry, Antonio, it won't happen again."

Really, am I just going to kneel down before my emperor? I'm not going to stand up and say how I feel inside.

I took another sip of my beer and diverted my attention to the game in front of me.

Antonio looked to see what I was looking at and said, "A baseball fan? Those Yankees sure are impressive, aren't they? Do you like sports betting? I have a place you can go to if you'd like to place some wagers over there."

I looked back at him and said, "Thank you, sir. I think I'm going to finish my beer, head upstairs, and relax for tonight."

Antonio let out a soft laugh, looked at my beer, and noticed I was almost done with it. He then said, "How about the next one is on me? Sit here, clear your mind, and watch some sports."

I nodded my head. Antonio got up from the chair and stood beside the lady talking to me earlier. Then I could hear Antonio say to the bartender, "Next beer is on me for that gentleman." As he pointed in my direction. Antonio then left the bar area.

I sat there looking at the TV, just letting all my thoughts fill my head again. I took a deep breath, lifted my head, closed my eyes, and released a long sigh of exhaustion.

Once I opened my eyes, I noticed that the lady from the bar was in front of me, sitting in the same seat as Antonio.

I thought to myself, oh great, here we go again.

She leaned in towards me and said, "You know the owner, that is super sexy. That means you must have some money." She looked at me with puppy eyes and said, "And you can buy this gorgeous lady a drink."

I shook my head no and said, "I'm sorry, lady, tonight I can't."

She then sat up straight and said excitedly, "How about I keep you company then? You look like someone that could use a friend right about now. I have a bubbly personality and can make you laugh all night."

Evelyn was the first thing that popped into my head when I heard her say that.

I quickly grabbed my beer so I wouldn't let a tear fall and took a sip. I don't need this lady seeing me at this point in my life like this.

I looked at the lady and exclaimed frustratedly, "Look, lady, I just want to be alone right now and drink my beer! Would you let me do that?!"

As I said that, some people in the bar area turned their heads to us. The lady had a shocked and hurt look on her face. I saw the look, and now I felt bad for raising my voice at this innocent lady.

Then I saw a tear falling from her eye, damnit, Will.

Why did you have to take it that far? You made this lovely woman cry; what kind of animal are you?

I grabbed my napkin and said, "Here, I am sorry for my outburst. I have had one of the roughest days ever, and I don't mean to take it out on you like that."

She grabbed the napkin, then grabbed a pen out of her purse and wrote something down on the napkin. Then she handed me the napkin, smirked, and said, "Here's my number. Call me if you change your mind and would like some company."

After giving me that, the lady got up from her chair, walked by me, stopped, and then put her hand on my shoulder.

She leaned in and whispered in my ear, "By the way, my name is Grace." Then proceeded to walk away.

Was all that just a simple act for me to lower my guard? I don't know what just happened, but I wasn't in the right mind.

I leaned back in my chair, looked up, closed my eyes, and let out another sigh.

I drank my beers and took a walk around the casino. There were so many machines than what Carlo's casino had. The tables looked clean and new.

I walked by a room that said, Texas Hold' Em above the doors. I thought to myself, I wonder what they do in there. I wanted to see what it was, but at the same time, I was scared to even venture someplace new.

That is how my whole career in this situation started. I shook my head no and said, maybe another time.

Then came upon an entrance with a name above it saying, Cosmic Zone.

This piqued my interest, so I entered through the doors and was greeted by two security guards. One of the guards said, "Hello, Mr. Bigsley, right this way."

I said to myself, Mr.? No one has ever called me that before. They probably are told to be very formal with everyone.

I walked into a dim room with curtains on each side, then the guard I was following opened the door to a club. It was dark, but the moving neon lights had enough light for me to see where I was going.

The music was so fast beat, and people were dancing all over the place. Some jumped up and down, and some had these glow sticks that made a cool look as they moved.

This place was insane and actually kind of awesome; I felt someone grab my arm, I looked to see who it was, and some lady said to me, "Dance with me!"

I saw a guard grab her and move her aside. I looked over at the guard with a confused look.

I thought to myself, she was only looking to have fun here.

We arrived at a table with three bottles of champagne in a bucket of ice. I looked around, and I didn't see anyone sitting at the tables.

I asked the guard, "Who's table is this?"

He replied, "This is yours, sir. Antonio told me to reserve a table for you in case you showed up."

"I don't want to stay here; I was just taking a stroll around the casino."

"Very well, I will get someone to put these back. What would you like to do, sir?"

I looked around, and people were everywhere. There was a couple on the wall in the distance making out. A group of people all jumping up and down to the beat on a dance floor. I could hear people yelling, "Go, go, go, go."

I turned to the guard and said, "Let's get out of here, and I want to finish the stroll."

We headed for the exit when my arm was tugged by another person. I looked back to see who it was, and Grace was the one pulling on my arm.

The guard approached her as if he was also going to move her aside.

I quickly said to him, "No, that's fine, you can leave her."

He released her from his arms and took a step back.

She approached me while biting her lip and said, "Quite the security you have there. Let's dance!"

I looked at my guard and said, "Wait for me by the entrance."

He nodded his head, and then walked away.

Grace leaned in and said in a flirtatious tone, "Were you following me in here? Do I have a stalker on my hands now that we met?"

I laughed as we both danced and said, "No, I was taking a stroll around the casino and came upon this place. It looked interesting, so I entered."

She looked at me with a confused look and said, "Don't you work for Antonio? You never knew this place existed? Where have you been?"

"This is actually my first day on the job. I was in a situation, and Antonio gave me a chance to prove myself, so I took it."

"That Antonio is such a nice guy, isn't he?"

I thought about the whole situation and Evelyn lying dead on the ground in front of me. He isn't a nice guy behind the mask, but I'm sure many people don't see that side of him. Only the side he needs to show to make his appearance prodigious.

I replied, "Yeah, he is a great guy!"

Even though I just thought about everything before saying this to Grace.

I looked at my phone to see what time it was. It was already a little past midnight, no wonder why I felt exhausted.

I leaned in and said to Grace, "I got to get out of here. I have an early morning tomorrow. If I get time, I'll call you so you will have my number. Oh, by the way, you never asked me for my name."

Grace giggled and replied, "That's because I know your name already, silly; it's Will."

I had a confused look; how does she know who I am without me telling her? Is she a spy for someone? Is this Carlo's doing?

Grace smiled at me, leaned in, and gave me a kiss on the cheek. Then said, "I will be awaiting your call tomorrow."

She turned around and walked away from me.

I stood there for a moment, confused about what had just happened.

Who is this lady? How does she know who I am? This thinking started hurting my head.

I turned and started walking over to the entrance. The guard opened the door for me and said, "Have a good day, sir."

I walked through the casino, still confused about this Grace lady. I had never seen her before in my life. All kinds of questions ran through my mind as I took every step.

My heart started to beat faster the more I thought about it. I said to myself, I need to get upstairs and go to bed before I overthink this whole situation.

I made my way through the crowd and casino. I arrived at the elevator to take me to my room.

Why does this elevator bring me back memories of what happened with Evelyn? How I stood there looking at my reflection.

The elevator opened up and took me upstairs to my floor. I walked over to my door, walked in, and lay in the bed with all my clothes on. I said to myself, this was an exhausting day. Hopefully, tomorrow is better.

Chapter 12

The next day, I woke up feeling refreshed. I got out of bed, stretched my arms in the air, and let out a breath of relaxation. I looked at the time, and it was 2:45 p.m. I thought to myself, I must have slept twelve hours.

I jumped in the shower, got ready for the day, and opened the curtains to let the sun hit my face. Then a thought occurred to me: I got abducted the last time this happened. I need to be cautious of how today plays out.

I went downstairs, and Grace was in the lobby seating area. I tried to dodge her as if she didn't see me, but she waved at me as I tried to move, and I wasn't fast enough to get out of the way.

I walked over to her and said, "Looks like I might have a stalker on my hands. I won't need to call you if we keep meeting like this."

She got up, and I noticed she was wearing a tight sky-blue mini skirt with high heels. And a halter top the same color as her skirt. I looked at the top she was wearing and noticed she didn't have the same physique as Evelyn, so there wasn't much protruding under her top.

Grace laughed and replied, "Yes, I am your stalker, and I'm here to take over your life."

I looked at her with a confused look. She must be here to kill me or something.

Grace started laughing again and said to me, "How was that? I am working on my acting skills to make it a career."

I replied, "I think some work needs to be added to emphasize the stalker part."

Grace laughed, nudged my arm softly, and said flirtatiously, "Oh, stop it. You are so funny, you know that. So, are you like living in the casino or something?"

"Since I agreed to work for Antonio, he told me I have an option of living here or at my home. Right now, I don't want to be at home, so I decided to live here for the moment."

"Why? What is going on at home that you don't want to be there?"

I thought about my answer for a moment. I don't want to tell Grace everything that has happened to me up till now. How do I answer this? How do I play the field, as they would say?

As I was thinking, Grace waved her hands in front of my face. She then asked, "Hello, is the house empty up there?"

I shook my head and replied, "I'm sorry I spaced out for a second. What was the question?"

Grace put her hand under her chin, one arm across her body, and looked at me. She proceeded to circle around me, looking at every side of me. Up and down, side to side. She poked my cheek a couple times.

I looked at her and asked, "What are you doing?"

"Oh, nothing much, just doing my own examination and assessment." She responded. "Once said examination is done, I'll decide if I will make you my boyfriend."

I shook my head in confusion. What did she just say? No! Definitely no! I don't need that in my life right now, and I can't afford to lose another person in my life. Everything has been falling apart since Karina left.

I grabbed her hands to hold them and said, "You seem very sweet and all, but I am not ready for any relationship. I need to focus on myself first. And how will you determine that without discussing something with me first? That means you make decisions on your own without communicating."

She turned away from me, crossed her arms, and said, "Fine, you bully. I don't want you to be my boyfriend anyways."

I put my palm up to my forehead and started shaking my head.

Why do I always end up in these situations like this? All I want to do is live the rest of my life stress-free without interruptions. Is that a hard thing to ask for?

Behind me, I hear a voice say in a southern accent, "So, you the one that has been keeping my girl warm at night."

I thought to myself, he can't be talking to me. The only person I've been keeping warm at night is myself. Not even myself, sometimes when I'm getting abducted. That felt like the person was behind, so I might as well see who they were talking to.

I turned around, and a man stood there staring at me.

I asked him, "Were you talking to me?"

"Yeah, are you the reason she ain't never came back to me?" The man said.

I met this lady the other day, and I'm already accused of stealing another man's woman. Can this day get any better?

Maybe I should have stayed in bed away from everyone.

The next time I wake up feeling amazing, I'm strapping myself to the bed and ensuring I don't go anywhere.

I replied, "I don't know what you're talking about, but I just me—."

Before I finished my sentence, Grace slipped in between the both of us. She yelled to the guy, "I thought I said never to come back here? Go back home to your miserable life and let me live mine. We have been done for quite a while now. So turn that large body of yours and make haste to the exit. DON'T... COME... BACK!"

The man went silent; I think I would too if this little lady would go off on me.

The guy turned his attention to me, pointed his finger in my face, and said, "Don't worry, this ain't over yet. I'll catch you again." He then turned and walked away to the exit.

Grace stood there with her hands on her hips and repeatedly tapped her foot on the floor. The way she managed that guy was kind of amazing. She has some balls under her skirt. Hopefully, not figuratively, I don't want to find a hidden surprise.

There was something about her that caught my eye. No Will! Turn away; no matter the fact, run away while you can. But she can manage her own, which is pretty hot.

Grace turned around to face me and gave me a huge, tight hug. I just raised my arms and didn't know what to do.

Do I hug her back?

Do I just let her hold me? Am I a teddy bear or something people need to hold on to like this?

Grace looked up at me with these eyes that could pierce a soul and said, "You're not going to hug me back?"

I quickly wrapped my arms around her and saw the devil horns returning to her head. Her wicked eyes turned into eyes filled with joy.

This is frustrating; she has complete control over me, and I never allowed it. I keep fighting it, but I'm on the losing end of this battle.

"So, what is on the agenda for today, boyfriend?" Grace said.

I replied, "I am not your boyfriend, and I don't know anything about you. You keep forcing this upon me, and I don't want a relationship right now."

I grabbed her arms to pull them off me and continued, "I have some things I must do. Have a good day."

She grabbed my arm and said, "I'll see you later."

I yanked my arm back and started walking away.

This is not good; I don't need to be in this situation. I need to find Antonio and see what he has for me today.

I walked outside to get some fresh air. The sun was still out and getting out of that casino felt good. I took a couple more steps forward, lifted my head, took a deep breath, and exhaled.

I said to myself, I need a vacation. A one-way trip to any place and just live there. Don't look back at this; leave all the stress behind me and start brand new.

As I became relaxed, I felt someone push me from behind hard. I fell into a column that supported the entryway. I shook my head to try and dust off the dizziness. I looked back, and that guy was back.

He yelled out, "I told you this ain't over. You ready for these hands to catch you?"

I looked at him, confused and trying to figure out what language he was speaking.

Catch hands? What does that even mean? I saw he had both hands up like he would hit me.

Is that what he means by catching hands?

The guy swung once, I ducked to get out of the way, and he missed. I reached back and punched him as he was still recovering from the swing, and I hit him directly on the side of the head, and he fell face-first into the ground.

That's it? One blast, and you're out? I thought I was going to have a hard time with this guy.

I turned around and started walking back to the casino until I heard him grunting and moaning. I turned back towards him, and he was trying to pull himself up. I shook my head and thought, this isn't good.

He recovered onto his feet and said, "That was a lucky hit; you ain't getting any more."

The guy started to rush at me like a bull. So, I moved out of the way, and he got punched in the face by Grace. The guy fell straight back onto the ground, twitching and screaming in pain.

I looked over at Grace and was impressed by that hit. That was a punch if I had never seen one, I thought. This girl definitely can hold her own, and I'm not trying to get into a fight with this chick.

Grace looked over at me and smiled. She then said, "You're welcome."

I said to her, "I had it under control."

She laughed and replied, "Oh yeah, it sure seemed like you did."

I walked over to her and said, "I guess thanks are in order for you."

Grace replied, "Are you ready to confess your love for me after watching me throw that haymaker."

This lady will not stop until she gets what she wants. She will bug me and bug me until she hears a yes come out.

I scratched my head in frustration and said, "You won't give up, will you?"

Grace replied, "Nope! Unless you're trying to end up like this guy."

She put her hands up as if she was going to hit me. I thought in my head, this lady better not be serious.

I grabbed her balled-up fists, brought her hands down, and said, "Okay, how about this. Give it time to get to know each other, and then I will say yes. But right now, it is still a no."

Before Grace could answer me, I heard my phone ringing. I looked and saw it was Antonio.

I said, "Hey, boss."

Antonio replied, "Are you busy tomorrow?"

"Not that I know of; why, what's up?"

"I have a special gift for you that you will love. Probably the best gift you would ever see from me. Meet me downstairs tomorrow, bright and early."

He hung up the phone, and I heard Grace say, "He must be more important than me?"

I laughed and said, "He's my boss; of course, I have to answer quickly."

"So, once I become the girlfriend, I'll become boss too. I will get answered faster, right?" Grace responded.

The only thing I could do was just stare in amazement that this lady was persistent.

I told Grace, "How about we get a drink and relax? I could use one right now."

Her face lit up like a Christmas tree when I asked her to get a drink with me.

She started to prance around and say out loud, "He asked me out! He asked me out! I can't believe it; he asked me out!"

I said to myself, lord, I have a child on my hands.

I reached out my arm so she could grab it and said, "Come on, let's go inside."

She quickly grabbed my arm with both of hers and started humming a merry tune as we entered the casino.

As we were walking inside, I turned to watch Grace walk. I felt comfort inside me with how she was next to me. I shouldn't be feeling anything from everything I have seen and been through. My body and mind should be numb to the world, but it wasn't.

I tried so hard with Evelyn not to let her in, but I fell for her after some time. I was hoping Karina would return to me during that time, but she never returned.

I wanted to take the easy way in life, and I only ruined it.

The one very thing I always remember my father telling me growing up was, "Son, to succeed in life, you have to earn your career. Don't ever try to take a way of life that was not destined for you. You can't cheat your way to the top. An honest man's work will pay off, but it might not be as soon as you want. But it is better than taking an easy way in life."

We arrived at the bar, and Grace asked me, "What do you want to drink?"

I was still in dreamland thinking about all that stuff and was not in my mind anymore.

Suddenly, I felt a pain in my chest; I returned to reality and noticed Grace's hand balled up on my chest. She just hit me! I guess that's what I deserve from not paying attention to her.

I said to Grace, "Owww. What was that for?"

Grace replied, "For you to come back to earth from outer space. Now, what do you want to drink, silly?"

"I'll have a beer," I said to the bartender.

We got our drinks and sat down at a table. Grace put both hands under her chin, had a smile on her face, and stared at me.

I thought she would ask me a question, but she just sat there and stared. It looked kind of creepy.

I asked, "Are you okay?"

She then asked me, "So, what did you do before joining Antonio? Were you married? Kids? Any exes I should be worried about? Any painful secrets you want to let loose on me?"

This lady does not hold back whatsoever. She has this bubbly personality but no filter at all.

Do I answer any of these questions truthfully?

Do I just throw a lie out there so she doesn't know my backstory? So many things ran through my mind as she asked me all these questions.

I answered, "I um… I… I—."

She stopped me and said, "Aye, aye captain." She let out this laugh that turned into a snort of some sort. I couldn't help but laugh with her.

While we laughed, I answered Grace, "I used to work at a dealership and made some decisions that weren't the best for my life. My girlfriend left me with our daughter at the time, and it started a downward spiral of events that landed me here."

I could not believe I had just answered her truthfully like that.

Did I do the right thing? I'm overthinking again; maybe Grace is a good girl that wants no harm done to anyone.

I asked Grace, "What is your story?"

She looked at me with these cute loveable eyes and said, "I am a stalker for a guy named Will."

She let out another laugh as before and snorted again.

She continued to say, "Oh my god, I crack myself up sometimes. I'm sorry, but I am just having fun today. I am regularly not this silly."

Looked down at the table and noticed she had finished her drink already. I asked her, "Do you want another one?"

She quickly nodded her head and replied, "Please! Thank you, you're so amazing."

I got up from the table and waited by the bar.

I tried not to make it look obvious, but I was looking in the corner of my eye to see what Grace was doing.

She pulled out her phone and had a stern face. I wonder what that is all about. She is not always about laughs and smiles. There is something behind the mask that I can't put my finger on.

I heard the bartender say, "What can I get you?"

I looked at the bartender and said, "I'll take another beer and whatever the lady was drinking."

The bartender went and got the drinks.

I wanted to look at what Grace was doing again. So, I tried to look in the corner of my eye again and noticed she was gone. I turned over to the table, and no one was there.

Where did she go? I barely turned away for two seconds to order our drinks. She couldn't have moved that quickly.

Then I felt a tug on my arm behind me. I turned around to see who it was, and Grace was pulling on my arm.

I was thrown off by how quick she moved behind me like that. She had this devilish grin and asked, "Were you looking for me?"

I said, "I turned to look over, and you were gone. I wanted to make sure that everything was alright."

She hugged my arm tighter, pulled herself closer to me, and replied, "I saw you looking out of the corner of your eye. You don't trust me, do you?"

I was stunned that she saw me doing that. I tried to be secretive about it, but that didn't work.

I know she is hiding something; I have a gut feeling that I am right. I need to expose it, but how? I feel that she is way smarter than me. How do I cut the corner and go around that?

She said, "Your story, which wasn't your true story, is it? Come on, let's sit back down and get to know each other for real."

We both sit back down at the table. We got comfortable, and Grace waved her hand in a circle in front of my face. As she did that, with a stern look, she said, "What are you hiding behind all of that."

The way she looked at me was very intimidating.

I took a deep gulp and said, "That story I told you is my real true story. Maybe some other time I can explain in detail the events that have happened to me. But for right now, I want to get to know who Grace is."

She leaned back in her chair, grabbed her drink, took a sip, and placed it down. She then leaned forward, put her elbows on the table, and said, "I don't tell many people this because they might get the wrong idea or think of me differently. I used to be a stripper, and I quit because I wanted to venture into the world. I want to see what the world has to offer me. So, I saved up my money before quitting, and here I am. Dun! Dun! Duuuuun!"

A stripper, huh? I must have a unique attractiveness to reel them into my life.

I took a swig of my beer and then placed it back down.

I leaned forward and gazed into Grace's eyes. Her blueish eyes were even more gorgeous, staring into them like that.

Grace slowly started to smile, and then a burst of laughter came out.

I asked her, "What's so funny?"

Grace finally stopped laughing and said, "I thought we were seeing who would blink first, and I did. So, that means I lost, and I couldn't help but laugh."

I thought to myself, maybe this is her authentic, bubbly self. She loves to have fun because having a serious face on all the time is no fun. We need to live a little and, in her case, a lot.

I sat there watching her have the time of her life. To live that free life that everyone needs to have every now and then. I could learn a lot from this lady.

I scooted my chair so I was next to hers, put my finger under her chin to lift her head, and leaned in for a kiss. Our kiss felt like it would last a lifetime. She placed her hand on my face and exerted more intimacy at the moment. She has the softest lips, I thought to myself as we kept kissing.

We stopped, and with a smile, Grace said to me, "You are an amazing kisser. But warn me next time, jerk!" Grace smacked the side of my arm to emphasize when she called me a jerk.

I gave into my feelings and asked Grace, "What are you doing tomorrow night? I am meeting with Antonio early morning, so I figured I would be available at nighttime."

She jokingly replied, "Hold on, let me get a hold of my secretary and see if I can fit you into my busy schedule."

I shook my head and said, "Really? Well, while you are at it, can you have your "secretary" pencil me in for all next week too?"

Grace looked at me with the most serious face I've ever seen her with, then turned into a smile. She then said playfully, "Stoooooop! You haven't had the chance to be with me one full night. You think you can maintain me for a whole week?"

I replied, "That's the plan."

What did I just do?

Am I living that free life that she is living also?

I think I just threw my rule book out the window and let whatever happens, happen. It feels good, but at the same time, I feel scared that I shouldn't be doing it.

I looked at the clock behind Grace; it was getting close to 10 at night.

I said to Grace, "I have an early morning. Let's plan on tomorrow night at my hotel room and have the time of our lives."

Grace had a sexy grin and said, "You better rest up. I am about to put you to work all night long. Possibly even blow your mind into outer space."

I got up from the table and walked to the elevator. That similar feeling I had when I was going to tell Evelyn how I felt came back. I had this nervousness, a dry mouth, and my heartbeat was beating rapidly. I hope I do not have a heart attack.

Maybe I should just head upstairs and get some sleep. This feeling might go away tomorrow morning.

The following day, I woke up, took my shower, and got ready for the day. I headed downstairs to meet up with Antonio.

I arrived at the lobby, and the receptionist said, "Hello, Mr. Bigsley. Antonio is waiting for you downstairs in room 123-c."

I made my way downstairs and saw Antonio with a big grin. Something about him was different, and he had a unique persona this time.

I asked Antonio, "So, what's the special gift?"

He gave me this evil snicker and said, "Just inside these doors. Follow me."

He opened the doors, and a person with a bag over their head was on the floor tied up. I had a sharp image appear in my head, and it was me under there, and I shook it off and kept walking forward.

Antonio let out a villainous laugh and said to the torturer in the room with me, "Let's unveil this villain and see who's under the bag."

The torturer walked over to the person on the floor and lifted the bag off. My eyes became big when I saw who it was.

I yelled out, "Carlo!"

The torturer ripped off some tape that was covering Carlo's mouth.

"Will, what are you doing here?" Carlo responded while catching his breath.

I shook my head in disgust, and Antonio let out the malevolent cackle as he had before.

Then he said to the both of us, "Don't you just love family reunions? They make you so warm and fuzzy inside."

Carlo repeated, "Will, did you hear me? What are you doing here?"

Antonio replied, "Well, don't keep your old boss waiting. He asked you a question, and please be polite to our guest."

Carlo looked at me in disgust and said, "Old Boss? What does he mean by that?"

Antonio excitedly said, "Oh, I forgot he still hasn't had a chance to tell you yet. Will, don't keep this man waiting now."

I replied, "They… they… kidnapped Evelyn and me in my house. Terrorized everything and brought us here. He gave me a choice to join him and that I would see Evelyn if I joined.

"I was going to tell her how I felt that night, and I loved her so much, Carlo! But they… they killed her already. Even after I decided to join and they threw her body on the floor in front of me."

Carlo's eyes became enraged, and he blurted out to me, "You bastard! You conniving bastard! What about the oath? Evelyn knew about the oath, and I am sure that's why they killed her. You are an idiot!"

Antonio butted in and said, "Oh yes, she didn't even put up a fight. I heard when they gave that option to her, she was a tough little cookie."

I looked over at Carlo and said, "I'm sorry, I wanted to see her again, and with hope, I thought I could."

Then I looked over at Antonio and yelled, "Let him go! You won, gained me, took out his other right hand, and there isn't anything left. LET HIM GO!"

Antonio looked at me with a confused face and said, "What do you mean there isn't anything left? There is plenty in store for me to go higher. And I won a battle but not the war. There is a lot for you to learn. Okay, I become a stamp on the Las Vegas strip.

"Everyone knows my name, but the world doesn't. I want world domination; I want the world to fear me. When they hear my name or see one of my buildings. I want those that defy me to say, "Let's not tread over these deadly waters." There is definitely more to achieve in life, Will."

Carlo looked over to me and repeated himself, "You bastard! I still can't believe you. How could you?!"

I stood there in disbelief that this had happened. How could I've been more stupid to not realize our oath?

Carlo was right, Evelyn knew what she had to do, and she did it. I wanted to see hope throughout and maybe a happy ending for me, and there was only one thing left to do at this point.

I said to Antonio, "You want to achieve all of that. Then I will help you succeed, but first, you must let go of this man." As I pointed to Carlo.

Carlo yelled out to me, "Don't be stupid, Will! I have lived my life and accepted death as my punishment!"

Then Carlo said to Antonio, "Do not listen to this... this BOY. Kill me and be done with me."

Antonio looks over at me with his hand under his chin and says, "So, you will help me achieve my goal if I let this man live, huh. Pretty brave of you to say, don't you think?"

"I said what I said," I responded to Antonio.

Carlo yelled out to me, "Damnit, Will! Don't you understand anything? Do not listen to this man. He isn't a giving man like I was, and he will slice your head off when you least expect it."

Antonio pulls out a gun and rushes over to Carlo. He points the gun at Carlo's head and says, "You would love for me to do the very thing you did to my cousin, right?"

Carlo killed Antonio's cousin, and this war had started over that. Each person has been hiding something from me, and I am still left in the dark.

I asked Antonio, "What did he do to your cousin?"

Antonio takes a step back, puts the gun back into his pants, and says to me, "Blake had brought a man to Carlo one day. He had said the very thing to you as he did to my cousin. Carlo took the man under his wing and brought success to his name.

"My cousin made one mistake, and Carlo ended his life like that." As he snapped his fingers and continued to say, "No explanation from my cousin, nothing. He was shot cold-blooded without my cousin telling his side of the story. This man is a murderer; he shot Blake because he knew something that the rest of us didn't. Isn't that right, Carlo?" He grabbed Carlo's face and pushed him back.

I looked at Carlo and asked, "Is he telling the truth, Carlo?"

Carlo looked at Antonio disgusted and then turned his attention towards me. He told me, "He knew something that he shouldn't have. He had that leverage on me, and I couldn't have that. So, I ended his contract."

Antonio says to me, "Now it all comes out. Do you still think this man deserves justice? Without hesitation, he killed an innocent man and felt no remorse for it."

I said, frustrated, "I am sure killing Carlo won't bring back your cousin. Whatever it was, I am sure the pain inside knowing what Carlo has done is slowly killing him."

Antonio rushes over to me, points the gun in my face, and says, "Maybe I should kill you for being a softy. I don't have any room on my team for someone like that."

Carlo blurts out, "He's right, Antonio. The pain inside me has been killing me softly and slowly, and I have hated myself for letting it get to that, and there is no going back from what I did."

"You guys are so pitiful," Antonio responds. "Maybe I should kill both of you and be done with it."

I got down on one knee, opened my arms wide, and said to Antonio, "If that's what you have to do, then so be it."

Antonio looks at me and then back at Carlo. He goes back and forth several times and screams, "ARGHHHH!"

He then walks over to the torturer and whispers something into his ear. I saw the torturer nod his head and walk out of the room.

He then comes back with a baseball bat and gives it to Antonio. The torturer picks up Carlo, so he is kneeling, and Antonio swings the bat at Carlo's head, knocking him out. He then gives a signal over to the torturer. He then unties the binds around Carlo and carries him out of the room.

I looked over at Antonio and asked, "What are you going to do with him?"

Antonio replied, "I am throwing him in a vehicle and having one of my men take him back to his casino so that he may be free."

He then points the bat at my face and continues, "You better not back out on your word. I will hunt you down, and it won't be pretty."

Antonio left the room, along with his other men. I stood there looking at the floor as if Evelyn still lay there. A tear fell from my eye when I started to think of how she held me at the house. I wanted that again; I wanted to feel her body on mine.

Is that why Grace feels so good to me when she's around?

I closed my eyes and visioned Evelyn walking towards me. I wanted to reach out to her, but I knew it wouldn't do any good.

I opened my eyes back up and found myself crying. I was emotionally drained from everything, and I knew I wasn't going to be able to see Grace like this.

I grabbed my phone and looked through my contacts. I came to Grace's name and wanted to call her. I need to cancel tonight, so I could regain my mind, but I didn't want to make her upset.

What do I do? I can't go on today with my mind like this.

I decided to hit the call button. It rang three times, and she picked up. I hear her say, "Hello, who is this?"

I forgot I never gave her my number, and I needed to answer quickly before she hung up.

I replied, "It is Will."

Her tone went from a defensive manner to a concerned style. She answered, "Hey, Will. Is everything alright?"

I tried holding back my sniffles from crying and said, "Yes, but can we reschedule for tomorrow night? The boss gave me a project that needs me tonight, and I want to make sure I am fully available for you."

She replied in an upset tone, "Okay, I guess I can wait."

"I'm sorry, but I will make it up to you. I promise!" I responded.

Then Grace said excitedly, "Yay! Can't wait to see you tomorrow!" Then hung up the phone.

I made my way back upstairs and into my room. I lay on the bed and just relaxed until I became tired and fell asleep.

Chapter 13

woke up in a puddle of sweat in the middle of the night, and I don't think I was dreaming or anything. I got up to look at the thermostat for the room; the temperature was at sixty-eight. My body felt hot, but it was cold in here.

What is going on?

Is this due to the stress I have been putting on my body? I have changed many living habits in the past couple of months, and something felt wrong.

I grabbed a water bottle that I had brought from the lobby and drank it. I felt slightly better after the water, but something still felt off.

I went to the bathroom and threw some water on my face.

Since I was still in the same clothes, I stepped out of the room and went to the lobby. From there, I made my way outside and towards the water fountain up front. I sat on one of the big rocks in front of the fountain and listened to the water flow.

I closed my eyes and let the sound relax my body and mind. The more relaxed I became, the more it felt like my body was floating in the air. I took a couple of deep breaths and exhaled, hoping this would change my state of mind.

With my eyes closed, I could hear the wind hitting the trees and moving the branches. The calming sound of the water flowing and the trees swaying helped me relax.

I could finally think clearly. Nothing seemed foggy in my mind, and I needed this setting more than anything.

I slowly opened my eyes and noticed a man sitting not too far from me, enjoying the soothing sounds with his eyes closed. All I could see was his closed eyes; I couldn't see what the rest of his face looked like.

With his eyes closed, he said, "There is no better sound in the world I would rather take in than this."

As I looked at him, I waved my arms in front of him, and he didn't even budge. The man added, "I don't need my eyes open to know that you are staring at me, waving your hand. I could feel your energy coming to me once you opened your eyes."

Who is this guy?

What is he talking about?

Then I replied, "Yeah, it was well needed."

He then opened his eyes and said to me, "Whatever it is that you're going through, just know that things happen for a reason. You can't challenge destiny to a duel and expect to win. What is meant to be will always find its way."

The man got up, walked over to me, placed his hand on my shoulder, and said, "Destiny has its ways of presenting itself to you. If you widen your horizon, expand your mind, and endure it in your heart. Then you shall possess its motives."

He then walked away and faded away in the night. I looked to see if I could find where he went but nothing. It is like he just vanished in thin air.

Was this man a figment of my imagination? I was confused, but something inside me felt relieved for some reason. My whole demeanor had changed, and I did not feel stressed anymore.

I took a deep breath in and exhaled. I got up from the rocks and went inside. I went to my room, laid back down, and fell asleep.

I woke up to the sun bearing down on my face. I looked at the clock, and it was a little past noon.

The thought of the guy telling me everything still lingered in my mind. I repeated what he said, "Destiny has its ways of presenting itself to you."

Is he trying to tell me something?

Or was he just a drunken man that was just blabbering on? He didn't smell like alcohol or liquor when he was next to me.

I jumped in the shower and let the water run down my head. I stood there staring at the floor for a moment.

Maybe I am just overthinking the whole situation. I could go for some food right about now.

I got out of the shower, put some clothes on, and drove to find a restaurant.

I let my mind take over me again while I was driving. I came to, looked in my rearview mirror, and noticed the light was red. Did I just run a red light? I need to stop spacing out like this.

I drove for a while, trying to find a place that looked good, and I just wasn't in the mood for anything. I wish Karina was still here; I could go for a lovely home-cooked meal.

I thought about driving back to Kingman, but I didn't want to see the house.

What should I do?

Where should I go? I got back on the road going back to The Enchanted Tomb casino.

I arrived back at the casino and went inside. I sat at the bar, asked for a beer, and ordered some food. A burger and fries caught my attention as I was exploring the menu. I sat back in my chair and watched the TV.

After I ate my food, I felt energized, and I could run a few laps and still feel good. I got up from the table and took another walk around the casino.

Antonio saw me and stopped me halfway into the casino.

He said to me, "Do you have a minute?"

I replied, "Yeah, I'm not doing anything."

"Let's talk in my office for a bit," He responded.

We walked into this area that was full of glass walls. I was in awe of how elegant the offices looked with the glass walls.

This was my first time ever coming this way. So, I did not know what to expect. We arrived at these tall double doors stained a bronze color with gold plated handles and features.

We walked in, and the mood of the room felt somewhat overwhelming. Antonio looks at me and says, "Have a seat."

Once we got comfortable, Antonio said, "How are you feeling? Can I still count on you to be there for me?"

I replied, "Of course. What is it that you need?"

Antonio said, "Those that seek success in life usually find it in their journeys. I want you to achieve greatness under me. I want to see you move up in this business, become someone, and mature as a powerful icon that people will recognize."

I had a confused look on my face as he was telling me this. I didn't know what to say or think.

Why is he telling me this all of a sudden?

Antonio continued to say, "I have a small project I have for you. It might be a little tedious but believe me, the outcome will be in your favor."

As he told me all this, I heard knocking on his door. Antonio got up from his chair and walked over to see who it was.

I could hear their conversation from where I was sitting. A man said to Antonio, "He's here, sir."

"He wasn't supposed to show until tomorrow," Antonio responded.

The man said, "All he said to me was, "Tell him I'm here, and I'm ready." He did seem a little irate when he said it."

Antonio replied, "Alright, tell him I'm on my way." Then shuts the door.

He walks over to me, puts his hand on my shoulder, and says, "Let's table this conversation for another day. But remember what I said, success is key to longevity in this business."

We both walked out of the office and back onto the casino floor.

Antonio turns to me and says, "It looks like you found yourself a new girlfriend, huh?" He pointed in a direction where Grace was standing and waving at me.

How did she know where I was?

Is she hired by Antonio to keep tabs on me? Something doesn't sit well in my mind.

"There you are, I asked a couple security guards if they had seen you, but only one told me where you were," Grace said.

She ran up to me and gave me a tight hug. She rested her head on my chest and remained there for a moment, and I was still in shock that she was standing there waiting for me.

She looked at me and asked, "Is everything alright with "the boss man"?"

I replied, "Yeah, we were just discussing about the future, success, and other stuff."

I stuck out my arm for Grace to grab and added, "Let's go for a walk."

She grabbed onto my arm and started humming a joyous tune.

While walking, she asked, "Are we still meeting tonight?

"Of course, I'm excited for tonight," I responded.

Grace said humorously with a smile, "You know, I told my secretary to clear my schedule for tomorrow so I could stay with you all night."

I looked at her and asked, "Do you really have a secretary?"

She puts her palm up to her forehead and shakes her head. She then says, "No, silly. I'm just being sarcastic. I wish I had a secretary, maybe one day."

We walked by a sitting booth, and Grace said to me, "Let's sit here for a moment."

We sat down, and Grace turned around with her back facing me. She scoots toward me and rests her back on me.

She then says, "Wrap your arm around me like this." She grabs my arm and places it around her sternum.

Grace takes a deep breath, lets out a sigh of relief, and then continues to say, "I could sit like this for days with you."

It was pretty comfortable sitting with her like that. I felt a feeling of security inside me, and I actually wanted this moment to last forever.

I still felt like there was something not right about Grace. She bonded with me too quickly that day at the bar.

After she saw Antonio talking with me, that's when her whole attitude changed. Maybe she is trying to go after Antonio and thinks she can get to him through me.

I couldn't resist, so I asked, "Why me?"

Grace laughed and said, "Why you what?"

"There were many others in the bar that day, but I was the lucky one out of all of them," I responded. "So, why me? What made me special enough for you to come up and talk to me."

She then rested her head on my shoulder and replied, "There was something about you that day that I saw. Like a glow or an aura as you walked into the bar area. It caught my eye, and I wanted to get more information about this sexy stud I saw. Besides, you looked like you had money, so I decided to pursue it."

I had a confused look and said, "Really, money?"

Grace laughed rambunctiously and replied, "Calm down, calm down. I was only kidding; well, about the money part. Everything else is true."

As we laughed, an older lady with her husband walked up to us and said, "There is something about young love that is so beautiful. Enjoy every moment, for time, is the enemy. You are young one day enjoying these marvelous moments. Then the next, you ponder the question, where did the time go? Can I take your picture, please? I would like to frame perfect moments like these. It reminds me of the energy my husband and I had when we were younger."

Grace looked at me with a big smile, then turned to the lady and said, "Of course, we would love that."

The lady was ecstatic that we agreed to the picture. She then said to us, "Thank you so very much! Have a blessed day." She then took our photo and walked away.

That was one of the best feelings I have had in a while. The exulting feeling definitely created a smile on my face.

Grace looked up at me and said, "That is probably the first time I ever saw you smile before."

"I smile, maybe not too often, but I do smile," I responded.

Grace laughed and said, "Not like that."

I replied, "You ready to go upstairs?"

Grace let out a long sigh and said, "I guess."

"We don't have to go yet. I just figured we get out of the casino floor." I responded.

She then said excitedly, "Oh no, I'm ready. Let's get out of here before more pictures are taken."

We both got up from the booth and headed to the elevator. Grace stopped me and said, "Oh wait, I have to go do something. I forgot I was supposed to do it before coming to the casino."

Grace let out a sigh of disbelief and continued to ask, "What room are you in? It will only take ten minutes, and I will be right back."

I replied, "Of course, do what you have to do. I am in room 517, the executive floor."

Grace said, "Okay, I'll be right back. Don't fall asleep on me now." She then ran off through the entrance.

Whatever she had to do, she sure took off quickly.

I made my way to my room and lay on the bed. I got up, looked around, and saw the place was a mess. What will she think when she walks into a pigsty of a room? I started getting all my clothes off the floor, wiping everything down in the bathroom, and ensuring everything looked nice and neat.

I looked around again and felt content with the way the room looked. Then I heard knocking on the door. Just in the nick of time, I said. I walked over to the door and opened it up. Grace had a small teddy bear holding a heart and a bag.

I asked, "Did you get me a teddy bear?"

"Well, who else are you going to cuddle when I'm not around," Grace responded.

She walked into the room and stopped in her tracks. She looked around and said, "You need a woman's touch here. How do men even live like this? I have a lot of work to do."

That is the same thing Evelyn said to me when she walked into the house for the very first time.

Why do I feel like this is déjà vu?

Come on, Will, snap out of it. Let us savor this moment. Look at the gorgeous lady in front of you. She is the reason that you are smiling and happy, right?

I walked up to her and grabbed the stuff in her hand. I threw them to the side, turned her around, so her back was facing me, and slowly started to kiss her neck so sensually. She grabbed the back of my head and pushed me closer to her neck. I had begun caressing her body, moving from her breast to her sides. I slowly lifted her dress up, embracing every curve on her body.

I could feel the goosebumps on her arms as they touched mine.

I got her dress lifted above her butt and kept going until it was entirely off. Her erotic moans in my ear were arousing and stimulating.

She repeatedly moaned my name as I kissed her neck, "Oh Will. Take me higher than the skies itself."

I threw her on the bed and started to undress. I was fully undressed, and she grabbed me to pull me closer. She laid me down with my back on the bed. She jumped on top of me, looked at me with a mischievous smirk, and said seductively, "Are you ready for me to... **blow your mind**?"

Before I could say anything, I heard a knocking on the door.

Oh great, not again. I looked at Grace, and she said, "You want me to get that for you?"

I replied, "No, they can wait!"

"Are you sure?" Grace responded.

I had a confused look on my face. Why does Grace want me to get the door?

What is behind the door that is more important than this?

I let out a small, frustrated scream, "Arghh!"

I moved Grace to the side, got my underwear back on, and said to Grace, "I will be back to finish this."

As I turned around to walk towards the door, Grace said, "I'll be waiting!"

I walked to the door, took a deep breath, and exhaled.

Okay, Will, be ready for anything.

I slowly opened the door, and my jaw dropped from what I saw. My eyes were opened wide, and I could not speak.

"Will, is Everything okay? Why are you in your underwear?" Karina said.

I couldn't respond right away. I was still shocked that Karina was standing right in front of me. I wanted to break down and cry where I stood.

The only thing I could get out of my mouth to say to Karina was, "What are you doing here?"

Karina replied, "I got Blake's text saying you were in trouble. That you were held up in some casino taken hostage. He said to come to the dealership, and we can go together. So I went over there, and it was empty, no cars, no lights on. Then I went over to the house, and it was demolished. What is going on, Will?"

Blake? He was shot before me, I got rid of his body, and I knew he wasn't alive. I am getting set up right now. Someone hired Karina to take me out; I know it, I can feel it.

I said to Karina, "That's impossible; Blake is dead! Carlo shot him before me. I haven't been taken hostage, nor do I plan to be. Well, right now, I'm not a hostage."

Karina looked into the room and saw Grace on the bed, naked. Grace humorously waved at Karina.

Karina looked back at me and said, "Who are you? You are definitely not the same Will I met when we were younger. I can't believe you're messing around with a... with a skank. Is this what you've been doing since I left you? You know what, don't answer that. I am taking Ashley and moving back to Minnesota. You will NEVER, EVER see your daughter or me again!"

Karina walked away, pissed off. I was in shock that this had happened. Karina finally returned to me, but this was not the way I wanted her to see me.

I slowly closed the door and went back to sit on the bed.

Grace got up and started to get dressed. I looked up at Grace with a confused look, wondering what was going on.

I asked Grace, "Where are you going?"

With a malicious cackle, she replied, "I just love it when plans fall together as they should! Revenge tastes great when victory becomes yours."

"What do you mean by revenge? I had never done anything to you that would make you seek retribution."

"Evelyn was the best thing that ever happened to me." She approached me, placed her hands on my legs, and continued to say, "She was my boss and best friend. Yet, you are still here, and she is gone. Now put that together in the equation. Then, you will get your answer. I have followed you since I saw you at the club meeting Carlo. Evelyn moved from the couch to your lap that day."

I dropped my jaw, and flashes of Evelyn popped in my head. The Last image that appeared was her lying on the floor after being thrown at me. I couldn't breathe anymore, and my body started to shake and shiver.

Then I said, "I didn't kill her; Antonio did when he abducted me."

Grace replied, "If she wasn't so busy trying to love you, she would still be alive."

She grabbed her stuff and took a couple of steps toward the door. She stopped in her tracks, turned around to face me, and with this heinous smirk, she said, "Oh, one other thing I forgot to mention. Carlo sends his regards. I was hired by him to get you into the perfect position."

What is she talking about? What perfect position is she rambling about?

Grace continued walking to the door, opened it, and left it wide open.

She was gone like Evelyn and Karina.

My life is ruined; I don't have a willingness to live anymore.

I saw two men enter the room and walk over to me from the corner of my eye. They both pointed a gun at me and then pulled the triggers.

The two men walked out, and my body hit the ground, making a thud sound. I lived this life because of greed and curiosity, and it got the best of me in the end.

Then I heard the words of the man by the fountain again. "What is meant to be will always find its way. Destiny has its ways of presenting itself to you."

A light shone over the man, and it revealed his face. That was me. That man had my face, and I was talking to myself, trying to give a warning.

It was fate! Fate had a purpose for being there that day. It was there to tell me to open my heart, see with my ears, and listen with my eyes. I didn't heed the warning; I was too obsessed with what filled my heart with desire, with lust.

This was my story and how it ended. Because my decisions and what I took for granted it swallowed me up; I couldn't fight back, I couldn't stand up and be the man I needed to be.

~THE END~

About the Author

I have always taken a liking to creating stories when I was younger. I used to play my video games and loved watching how everything unfolded. After many years passed by, I decided to fulfill that passion and created something start to finish. The feeling of accomplishment was real after I finally sat back and gazed over my work.

In school, I never paid attention to grammar or punctuality. When I started this book, I went over many documents online and taught myself many things I never knew existed. If only my English teacher could see me now, she would be proud and amazed at my wonderful accomplishments. I am not going to stop there though. I want to continue to construct amazing novels and stretch my mind to see what I can conjure.

When I created Evelyn's character I was fascinated by it. The more I developed her, I wanted to get to know her more. So, I am composing a book about her life of how she started until the events of this book introduced her. Keep an eye out for this amazing book titled, Evelyn.

Let me know what you think; You can find me on:

Facebook: Tomas M. DeLaCruz

Twitter: @TomasMDeLaCruz

Made in the USA
Monee, IL
02 June 2023

35137524R00127